OTHER YEARLING BOOKS YOU WILL ENJOY

FAST FORWARD: A DANGEROUS SECRET, *Ian Bone*

CHIG AND THE SECOND SPREAD, *Gwenyth Swain*

THE GYPSY GAME, *Zilpha Keatley Snyder*

WITH LOVE FROM SPAIN, MELANIE MARTIN
Carol Weston

BLUBBER, *Judy Blume*

THE UNSEEN, *Zilpha Keatley Snyder*

BOYS AGAINST GIRLS, *Phyllis Reynolds Naylor*

MOLLY MCGINTY HAS A REALLY GOOD DAY
Gary Paulsen

attaboy, Sam!

LOIS LOWRY

Illustrated by Diane deGroat

A YEARLING BOOK

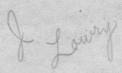

Published by Yearling, an imprint of Random House Children's Books
a division of Random House, Inc., New York

Visit us on the Web! www.randomhouse.com/kids

Educators and librarians, for a variety of teaching tools, visit us at
www.randomhouse.com/teachers

ISBN: 0-440-40816-4

Reprinted by arrangement with Houghton Mifflin Company

Printed in the United States of America

July 1993

22 21 20

attaboy, Sam!

S*A*M

1

"What on earth are you doing, Sam?" Mrs. Krupnik stood in the doorway staring at her son. Sam looked up.

Moms were sometimes very strange, he thought. They always asked what you were doing, even though they could *see* what you were doing.

Once, when he was younger and naughtier, Sam had found it interesting to unroll toilet paper. He knew that he wasn't supposed to. But every time he wandered past the bathroom and glanced in and saw that roll of paper hanging there, with its end dangling in a tantalizing way, he couldn't seem to stop himself. He would have to go in and unroll it. If he got it going just right, he could twirl the roll around very fast, and the paper would go all over the floor, and it was wonderfully interesting to him.

1

And always, whenever he did that, his mom would appear in the bathroom doorway and say, "Sam! What on earth are you doing?"

He could never figure it out. What did she *think* he was doing — taking a bath? Brushing his teeth?

Today, though, he wasn't unrolling toilet paper. He was much too old to do a baby thing like that.

Today he wasn't even in the bathroom. He was in the study. His dad's study. He looked over at his mother, who was still in the doorway. Then he said patiently, even though he was quite certain she knew exactly what he was doing, "I'm typing."

She came across the room and stood behind him, looking down over his shoulder. "My goodness," she said. "You really are!"

Good, she didn't sound angry. She sounded surprised.

Sam didn't know why his mom would be surprised that he was typing. His father's typewriter, here in the study, was a fascinating thing. And his dad had showed him, once, how you rolled in a piece of paper and then pushed the keys with letters on them.

"I typed my name," Sam told her with pride.

And he had. *sam   sam   sam*

He had made some mistakes, of course, since it was his first try at typing. One of his *sam*s had come out *sal* and another said *wam*.

But he was getting better at it.

"Look," he said. Very carefully, with his tongue wedged between his teeth, he typed *mom*. Then he rolled the paper a bit in order to start in a fresh place.

"Attaboy, Sam!" his mother said. "You're an absolutely amazing son!"

Mrs. Krupnik pulled up a chair beside Sam and showed him all sorts of interesting things: how to make big letters, so that he could type *SAM* instead of just *sam*. How to make little stars, *****, so that he could now type *S*A*M* and *M*O*M*.

She showed him how to make a sideways smiling face:

:)

Then Sam figured out, all by himself, how to make a sideways grumpy face:

: (

And together he and his mom discovered how to do a sideways *winking* smiling face:

;)

Finally, when the page was filled, Sam took it out of the typewriter and gave it to his mother.

"That's fabulous, Sam," she said. "I'll stick it on the bulletin board in the kitchen. Now, how about lunch? I cooked some hot dogs."

Sam trotted behind her down the hall to the kitchen and watched with pride while she thumbtacked his typing paper to the bulletin board next to a painting of a rainbow he had done in school.

"I want mustard on my hot dog," he said. "Yellow mustard, not brown. And ketchup. And also I want a pickle, and three cookies, and I want chocolate in my milk, and after that, an apple."

His mother, smiling, arranged all of those things in front of him on the kitchen table. As Sam began to eat, he glanced over at the refrigerator door, where his magnetic plastic letters had lived for months. SAM, they said, in yellow and green, and LOOK in red and blue.

It was the magnetic letters (helped along by his mom, dad, and big sister) that had taught him the sounds of the letters.

"After lunch," Sam announced, "I'm going to take all my letters off the refrigerator and throw them away."

"Throw them away? *Why?*" Mrs. Krupnik asked.

Sam thought about it. He made a new decision. "No, not throw them away," he said. "I'll give them to babies. Maybe to the kids at my nursery school. Because now that I'm a typer, I don't need baby stuff like those letters anymore."

"Gosh," his mother said, "if you're so grown up that you don't want your plastic letters anymore, maybe we should think about giving away your toys, too. Maybe, instead of your Matchbox cars

5

and your Lego set, you'd rather have a briefcase and a box of cigars."

Sam thought about that. He pictured how it would be to show up at nursery school some morning carrying a briefcase and smoking a cigar. Maybe he would take a bottle of beer, too.

It sounded like a great idea. But he had a feeling that Mrs. Bennett, his nursery school teacher, wouldn't like it much. She'd probably say, "Time out, Sam," and he would have to sit in the big green chair, drinking his beer and smoking his cigar all alone while the other kids were doing something fun, like fingerpainting with chocolate syrup or spelling their names in macaroni.

He smeared the ketchup and mustard together along the top of his hot dog with one finger. Then he licked his finger carefully.

"No," he said. "I think I'll keep my toys for a while."

"Good," his mother said. "I'm glad you decided that, because I hate the smell of cigars."

"Not pipes, though," Sam pointed out. "You don't hate the smell of pipes, do you?" He tried holding his hot dog like a pipe, but it bent in the middle.

"Well, no," his mother admitted, laughing. "I wish your dad didn't smoke at all, because it's bad for him. But I do love the smell of his pipe. As a matter of fact, I think I can smell it right now, coming up the back porch steps. Dad and Anastasia must be home from the store."

"Hi, guys," Sam's sister, Anastasia, said as she entered the kitchen. She set a grocery bag on top of the washing machine and went to hang up her jacket.

"I hope you made more of those hot dogs," Sam's dad said. He put his two grocery bags on the counter beside the refrigerator. "Shopping makes me hungry. I bought a whole lot of stuff we don't even need just because I was hungry."

Mrs. Krupnik groaned as she peered into one of the bags. She made a face. "Frozen enchiladas?" she asked. "That wasn't on my list."

Sam's dad shrugged. "They looked good," he said. "I *told* you: I was hungry, and I lost control."

Mrs. Krupnik sighed, wedged the frozen enchiladas into the freezer beside the ice cube trays, and prepared hot dogs for Mr. Krupnik and Anastasia.

"Bad news," Mr. Krupnik announced when he was seated at the table and had decorated his hot dog with mustard.

Sam wiggled in his chair and listened intently. Sam loved bad news. It was always much more interesting than good news. Sometimes, usually at breakfast, he listened when his parents read newspaper headlines aloud to each other.

7

Good news was boring, like: "Harvard Physicist Wins Nobel Prize." Sam didn't even know what that meant, though his parents seemed to, and even Anastasia, who was thirteen, squealed, "Hey, that's Norman Berkowitz's father!" Ho-hum, thought Sam.

But bad news was something else. Bad news was like: "Train Crash Injures 47." Or: "Bridge Collapse Leaves Terrified Motorists Stranded." Sam always listened carefully to bad news; it was just as good as listening to Mrs. Bennett read a scary story about monsters. It made you shiver a little.

"What is it? What's the bad news?" Sam asked, since his dad was chewing his hot dog and had forgotten to tell.

"Well," Mr. Krupnik said sadly, "This morning I went to Lord and Taylor's to get your mother some perfume for her birthday — "

Anastasia interrupted him with a giggle. "Dad *hates* going to Lord and Taylor's!"

"That's true," Mr. Krupnik acknowledged. "But I did it, Katherine, because your birthday is coming, and I went to the perfume department, which is the *worst*, in terms of geography."

"Why?" Sam asked. "What's worst about it?"

Anastasia explained to her brother. "In order to get to the perfume department, you have to walk through Lingerie and Nightgowns. Dad hates that."

8

"Is that the bad news? What's lingerie?"

"Underpants and bras," Anastasia explained impatiently. "Dad hates walking through underpants and bras."

Sam shrugged. It didn't seem like such a big deal, walking through underpants and bras. He would do it if he had to. Sometimes he *did* do it, in the kitchen, when the laundry was on the floor in front of the washing machine. He walked through underpants, and bras, and nightgowns, and T-shirts, and blue jeans, and everything else, and he thought it was fun.

"What *is* the bad news, Myron?" his mother asked.

"No more Je Reviens," Mr. Krupnik said sadly. "I was going to get you some for your birthday, but the salesgirl said that they don't carry it anymore."

"Oh, no!" Sam's mother wailed. "That's the only perfume I've worn for years!"

"Don't worry, Mom, we can find you some other perfume. Maybe it's time for a change anyway," Anastasia said reassuringly.

Sam almost yawned, he was so bored. "I'm done," he said. "Can I be excused?"

"May I be excused," his mother corrected automatically. "Yes, you may. Let me wipe your hands; they're all mustardy." She reached across the table with her napkin and wiped the bright yellow smears from Sam's hands.

Sam wandered out of the kitchen while his parents and sister were still talking about perfume. He began thinking about birthdays. His mother's birthday was next week.

She had told the whole family that she really truly didn't want fancy gifts for her birthday — except for a new bottle of perfume, because her old one was almost empty. What she *really* wanted, Katherine Krupnik had announced, was homemade things. She liked those best. She still had, in the studio attached to their house where she worked on illustrations for children's books, a little clay paperweight that Anastasia had made for her years before.

So Sam was making her a card at nursery school. It was purple construction paper, and he was pasting gold hearts on it; inside, he planned to write MOM and SAM and LOVE, and maybe he would also write HAPPY BIRTHDAY if there was room and if Mrs. Bennett would spell it for him. And probably, too, he would draw a dinosaur.

He knew that Anastasia was planning to bake a cake and that she would let him help frost it and set up the candles.

But now, climbing the stairs to his room, where he had been working for several days setting up a complicated speedway for his cars and trucks, Sam began thinking about perfume.

His mom needed new perfume. She *wanted* new perfume. But the store didn't have the kind she wanted. They didn't make her kind anymore.

But I could, Sam thought. I'm probably the only person in the world who knows all of Mom's favorite smells. If I start collecting them now and putting them together, it would take me about a week, and then, just in time for her birthday, I would finish. What a surprise! A special perfume, invented by Sam Krupnik!

Shaking his head in amazement at what a wonderful idea he had had, Sam entered his bedroom. He knelt on the floor by his speedway and halfheartedly moved a dump truck from one place to another, making room for an ambulance to enter from a side road.

But he wasn't really thinking about his speedway at all. He was thinking about how to begin his perfume. He remembered his mother saying, just a few minutes earlier, "I love the smell of your dad's pipe."

Pipe smell would be the starting place. He would start as soon as no one was looking, because it was going to be a surprise.

Sam grinned. Attaboy, Sam, he said to himself with satisfaction.

2

With his mom's birthday only a week away, Sam had no time to lose.

First, he knew, he had to find a container. Collecting smells for perfume would be useless if he had no place to keep them.

He looked around his room. On his windowsill, next to a plastic He-man, a coffee can held his crayons. It had a nice tight plastic lid and said Chock Full O' Nuts on the side; beneath those words it said COFFEE, in red letters on a yellow background.

It made a very good crayon can. But Sam had never been able to figure out what Chock Full O' Nuts meant, and his mom didn't know, either.

They had discussed it several times and finally decided that maybe the can had started out as a can for peanuts or cashews, but later the people at the factory changed their minds, so they added the word COFFEE in red letters, but they forgot to erase that stuff about nuts.

The can was just the right size for mixing perfume. And he *could* dump out the crayons, he knew. But Sam really didn't want his mom's birthday perfume to end up in a can that said Chock Full O' Nuts on the side.

He decided to check out his sister's room.

"Anastasia?" he called, standing at the foot of her stairs. Anastasia's bedroom was on the third floor, in a sort of tower that stuck out on the side of their big, old house. Sam thought that his sister was very lucky to have a tower room, and sometimes he *sort of* wished that he could live in a tower, too, but not really, because it might be scary at night.

"What?" she called back.

"Can I come up? I mean, may I come up?"

His sister was awfully fussy about people coming into her room without permission. Sam could understand why. When he was younger (and therefore dumber, and therefore naughtier), he had occasionally messed up her stuff when she wasn't home. Like he had dumped her goldfish down the

13

toilet. And he had spilled a glass of grape juice on her desk, over her homework. He had tasted all her Magic Markers and left the caps off. Once, when she had a cage full of gerbils, he had —

Well, Sam didn't like to think about stuff like that. Now that he was older and wiser, he *always* asked permission to enter Anastasia's room.

"Sure," she called back. So Sam climbed the stairs.

"What're you up to?" Anastasia asked. She was seated at her desk, writing in her journal. It was a green notebook, and very private, Sam knew. No one in the family was allowed to read Anastasia's journal. She had told them all that it was booby-trapped, and that there were invisible hairs across the pages so that she would know if it were ever opened by someone else.

Maybe there was even a bomb attached to it, Sam thought. He would never *ever* look in Anastasia's private notebook. "I'm not up to anything," Sam said. "How's Frank?"

Anastasia glanced over at the goldfish bowl where Frank swam slowly around in circles. His full name was Frank the Second. Frank the First was the one that Sam had flushed down the toilet.

"He's okay, I guess," Anastasia said. "He ate a pretty good breakfast this morning."

Sam watched Frank for a moment. "He's kind

of boring," he said. "All he does is swim and eat, swim and eat. And sometimes he moves his lips, like he's kissing."

Anastasia nodded. "Goldfish are *quite* boring," she whispered. "I wouldn't say that real loud, because I don't want to hurt Frank's feelings."

Sam sighed. "I wish we could have an *interesting* pet," he said.

"Shhhh." Anastasia gestured toward Frank. She held her finger to her lips, to indicate to Sam that he should whisper so that Frank wouldn't overhear.

"I wish we could have an interesting pet," Sam whispered.

"The Sheehans are giving their kittens away. Free food, too," Anastasia told him. "But you know what the problem is. *Dad.*"

Sam frowned. "Dad's 'lergic," he said.

"Well, he says he is. Mom thinks he's just imagining it. But years ago, before you were born, I had a cat, and Dad had a sneezing attack, so we had to give it away."

"Poor you," Sam said sadly.

"Poor me," Anastasia agreed. "And poor *cat.* I gave it to some neighbors who promised they'd take wonderful care of it, but they didn't, and a week later it got run over by a car."

Sam and Anastasia sat silently for a moment,

feeling sorry for themselves, and for cats, and for Frank, who only swam and ate and swam and ate and was boring.

Then Sam remembered why he had come to his sister's room. "I'm looking for a container," he said. "Do you have a container I can use?"

Anastasia wrinkled her forehead. "A container for what?"

"Secret," Sam told her. "I can't tell. I'm making Mom a birthday present."

"A box?" Anastasia asked. "There's an empty shoebox on my closet shelf. My new sneakers came in it."

Sam thought for a moment. A box wouldn't work for perfume, he decided. He shook his head.

"I need a bottle," he explained. "Or maybe a can."

"Look in the recycling barrel in the pantry," Anastasia suggested. "That's where all the empty bottles and cans go."

Sometimes Anastasia was a terrific sister, Sam thought. He gave her a high-five and turned to leave.

"Know what?" she said. "I'm making Mom a birthday present, too."

"Is yours secret, like mine?" Sam asked.

She shook her head. "No, not really," she said. "It's stupid, though. I'm writing her a poem."

"Why is it stupid?" Sam asked. "I like poems. My favorite is 'I'm Popeye the sailor man, I live in a garbage can' —"

Anastasia interrupted him. "It's stupid because I'm not a good writer," she said with a sigh. "Listen to this, Sam, and tell me what you think." She took a piece of paper from under her journal and read:

I'm glad that you've become 38
And that your name is Katherine, not Kate
And that Myron Krupnik is your date

She looked up, embarrassed. "I know it's stupid," she said sheepishly. "It's really stupid to say Dad is her date. But husband doesn't rhyme."

Sam thought about it. He *did* think the poem was a little stupid, but he loved his sister and didn't want to tell her so. "You could say Myron Krupnik is her *mate*," he suggested finally.

Anastasia brightened. She crossed out *date* and wrote *mate* in its place. "Thanks, Sam," she said enthusiastically. "You've given me a fresh view of it."

Sam headed down the stairs and made his way to the pantry on the first floor.

Anastasia had been correct. The plastic trash barrel in the corner of the pantry was filled with empty cans and bottles. Sam peered down the hall to make certain that his parents weren't nearby

17

and wouldn't appear suddenly to ask him what he was doing. But he could hear the announcer's voice from the football game on the living room TV, so he knew his dad would be lying on the couch, calling out, "All *right!* Go for it!"

He could hear his mother's footsteps in her studio. Today was Saturday, and usually she didn't work on Saturdays. But he knew that she was hurrying to finish a book about snails in a garden and that she only had the most boring part — the cabbages — left to do. He figured she was in there doing cabbages.

Sam looked carefully through the cans and bottles. It was important, he knew, to start with a container that smelled good. There were a couple of empty beer bottles — Miller Lite — but he decided against them. If he were making perfume for his dad, a Miller Lite bottle would be a good container. But his mom, he knew, didn't much like the smell of beer.

He thought long and hard about a peanut butter jar that still had a thick rim of peanut butter inside it. His mom *did* like peanut butter, Sam knew. But he decided against the Jif jar. He was afraid it wouldn't be large enough.

Finally he settled on a huge empty bottle that had held grape juice and still had some pretty good purple at the bottom.

Quietly, so that no one would hear him go by in the hall, Sam carried the grape juice bottle to his room and hid it inside his toybox.

In his mind, Sam renamed his toybox. He would call it the Lab. A lab, Sam knew, was a place where scientists invented important stuff.

Next, he crept downstairs again and into his father's study. He stood very still, near his father's desk, and listened. From the living room, he heard the TV roar of cheering crowds and the announcer's voice saying something about a field goal. From the studio, he could hear music start; he knew that his mom had turned on her little radio. She was definitely, Sam decided, working on cabbages.

Sam climbed into his father's chair — the same chair where he had knelt to do his typing just that morning — and leaned across the desk to inspect his father's collection of pipes. He sniffed. The smell of pipe — the same smell that his mother said she loved — was very strong.

He knew that he couldn't take one of his father's spectacular pipes: not the one carved into the shape of a hand, with its knobby fingers like a fist; and not the one with a face chiseled into the rounded end. His dad would notice if those special pipes disappeared.

Thoughtfully Sam selected a very ordinary-looking pipe: a brown one with a straight black stem. He sniffed it to be certain that it had a good pipey smell, and he peered inside it to be certain that there were flecks of tobacco in the bowl.

He put it into the pocket of his jeans. Then he strolled out into the hall, wearing his "Who, me? I'm not doing anything naughty" face. No one appeared. There was no one around to look at him suspiciously. From the living room door he could see that his dad was half asleep in front of the TV.

Sam scampered up the stairs to his bedroom. He closed his door, went to the corner where the Lab was, opened the lid of the grape juice bottle, and dropped in the pipe. He looked at it for a moment, thinking. Then he got a glass of water from the bathroom, and with great care he poured the water over the pipe, tobacco, and grape juice. Then he screwed on the lid of the bottle, closed the wooden lid of the Lab, and grinned.

It was a great start: the perfect smell of pipe.

Now he had to figure out what to add next.

3

"Anastasia," Mrs. Krupnik said at dinner that evening as she heaped chicken stir-fry onto plates and passed them around, "Mrs. Parish called earlier, while you were at Daphne's house. She wanted to know if you could babysit with Alexander for a while tomorrow afternoon."

Anastasia groaned and made a face. "What did you tell her?" she asked.

"I told her you'd call her back, of course. I told her I thought you didn't have any plans for tomorrow, but I didn't want to promise without asking you."

"I hate babysitting," Anastasia said. "But I need the money. I wish there were other ways for people my age to earn money. I wish I could be a part-time librarian, or something. Is it only for a little while, are you sure?"

Mrs. Krupnik shrugged. "That's what she said. Maybe an hour and a half. He'll probably sleep the whole time."

Anastasia poked at her dinner. "Okay. I'll call her after I'm finished eating."

Sam wasn't paying much attention to their conversation. He thought babies were very boring. At his nursery school, the girls all played complicated games with dolls, dressing them and undressing them, putting them to bed, feeding them fake food, taking them for walks in doll carriages. Sam thought it was really weird, playing that.

Sometimes Mrs. Bennett said, "Boys, it's okay for you guys to play with the dolls, too, you know. Because when you grow up, maybe you will be daddies. And daddies feed babies, and give them baths, and take them for walks."

Sam knew that. In the Krupniks' photograph album, there was even a picture of his dad giving him a bath when he was a baby. There was water all over the floor, and Sam was holding a toy duck.

So sometimes, at school, Sam tried playing with the dolls. But the girls got mad at him. They yelled and cried and said that they didn't *want* the babies to be named Rambo and Donatello. They didn't *want* the babies to drown in the bathtub or to be exploded out of the doll carriages.

And if you couldn't do those things, Sam thought, then it didn't seem like much *fun,* taking care of babies or playing with dolls. Not when there were trucks and airplanes to play with. Not when there were blocks that could be built into high towers and then knocked down with wonderful crashing sounds.

So he just continued eating his chicken, smooshing one finger in some sauce that had spilled over the side of his plate, and he didn't bother listening to his mom and sister talking about babysitting.

Until his mom said this very weird thing: "I just love the smell of little babies."

Sam looked up.

Anastasia made a face. "The *smell* of little babies?" she said.

Mrs. Krupnik nodded. "I went over to the Parishes' the other morning, when you guys were at school, because I'd bought them a baby present when Alexander was born. But I somehow never got around to taking it over, and now, my goodness, it's been more than two months. So I went over to deliver the gift, and the baby was awake — Nancy Parish had just bathed him — and I suddenly remembered how much I've always loved the smell of new babies."

"I love the smell of stir-fry," Mr. Krupnik said, reaching for a second helping.

"Here, have some more rice, too," his wife said, and heaped some on his plate. "Anyway, I sat there with sweet little Alexander up against my shoulder, smelling of powder and baby shampoo, and I rocked him, and it brought back some really nice memories."

Anastasia began playing an imaginary violin. Her mother looked at her and laughed.

"Would you say that it's your *best* smell?" Sam asked his mother.

"What do you mean?"

"I mean, your *favorite* smell?"

She nodded. "Well, I'd call it *one* of my favorites," she replied.

That was all Sam needed to hear. "Anastasia," he asked politely, "can I go with you when you babysit with sweet little Alexander?"

"May," Anastasia corrected patiently.

"*May* I?" Sam asked.

Anastasia sighed. "I suppose so," she said. "If Mrs. Parish doesn't mind. I'll ask her when I call."

The Parishes lived very near the Krupniks, in the middle of the next block. Sam trotted along the sidewalk beside his sister. He kept one hand in the pocket of his corduroy jacket, where he was carrying a neatly folded Ziploc bag.

He couldn't quite picture exactly how he was going to collect the smell of Alexander. The pipe had been easy, because it was a *thing*. But of course he couldn't bring a piece of Alexander home. He would have to collect the baby's smell, somehow. A Ziploc bag seemed necessary.

"Look," Anastasia said, pointing, as they passed the Sheehans' driveway. Sam looked and saw a large cardboard box with a sign on its side.

"Can you read it?" Anastasia asked. "Want me to read it to you?"

"No, wait," Sam told her. He began to make the sounds of the letters.

"Ffffff," was the beginning sound.

"Rrrrrr," was the next.

"Eeeeeeeeeeeeee," Sam said third.

"FREE!" he announced. He didn't bother with the second word on the sign. If the first word was FREE, then the second word didn't matter much. He ran up the driveway to the box.

It was just what Anastasia had told him. *Kittens!* He and his sister peered into the box and watched the five kittens scampering inside, chasing each other's tails and batting each other with their paws.

They watched in delight until Anastasia noticed the time and told Sam they would have to hurry on to the babysitting job.

" 'Bye, kittens," Sam said turning away from the box. "I wish Dad wasn't 'lergic," he said sadly as he trudged along beside his sister.

"I won't be gone very long," Mrs. Parish told them when they got to her house. "My husband's giving a talk at the Museum of Fine Arts, about Etruscan pottery. I told him I'd come and applaud at the end, just in case no one else does.

"Alexander's sound asleep," she said, and led them to the baby's room. "If he wakes up, Anastasia, his bottle's in the fridge, same as it was last time you were here. And you know where his diapers are."

Anastasia smiled and nodded politely. Sam could tell from the way she smiled — it was a fake smile — that his sister sincerely hoped that Alexander would not wake up.

Sam edged close to the crib, his face against the bars, and peered in. The baby was on his back, with both arms outstretched. His mouth was open a little, and there was a bubble of spit at one side of it. The spit bubble moved up and down slightly as Alexander breathed.

Sam sniffed. He couldn't smell anything at all.

He moved along the length of the crib so that he was closer to Alexander's head. He sniffed again.

"Your brother doesn't have a *cold*, does he?" Mrs. Parish asked a little apprehensively.

"No," Anastasia replied. "I don't know why he's doing that. Why are you making that noise, Sam?"

Sam thought quickly. He knew he couldn't say to Mrs. Parish, "I'm smelling Alexander." She wouldn't understand that at all.

"Sorry," he said. "I was making rhino snorts." He pointed to the corner of Alexander's crib, where a stuffed rhino was propped on its fat hind legs. It had a thick white plush horn coming out of its nose and a sewn-on smile below.

Mrs. Parish laughed. She turned to leave the room, talking to Anastasia, handing her a paper with the museum's phone number. Sam sniffed one more time, deeply, but smelled nothing. He followed them from the room, disappointed, touching the Ziploc bag in his pocket with concern.

"I knew it," Anastasia muttered. "I *knew* it!" She put down the magazine she was reading.

Sam looked up from the television; he'd been watching a nature show about frogs. When he pressed the Mute button on the remote control, he could hear Alexander quite clearly. Alexander was howling.

The sound made Sam nervous. One of the good things about the dolls at nursery school was that they couldn't cry. If you wanted them to cry, you had to make the wailing sounds yourself, and that was fun because it gave you a reason to howl and scream. But it wasn't scary at all. It *was* a little scary, listening to Alexander howl.

"What should we do?" he asked his sister.

She patted his head reassuringly. "*You* don't have to do anything, Sam. You can watch 'Frogs of the Amazon.' Me, I have to heat up his bottle, change his diaper, feed him — if he wants to eat, which he doesn't, always — rock him, pat his back, talk stupid baby talk for a while, and then, if he doesn't stop crying — though he *might*, if we're lucky — I'll have to implement my Never-Fail Baby-Soothing plan, which is a big pain in the neck, but it always works."

"Can I watch? I mean, may I?" Sam asked.

"Sure," his sister said. "But 'Frogs of the Amazon' is more interesting."

Sam thought that was probably true. But if he was going to capture Alexander's smell, he needed to be right there, on the scene.

He watched Anastasia start the bottle warming in the kitchen. Then he followed her to the baby's room and watched as his sister uncovered Alexander, who was kicking his legs and flailing his arms and screeching.

Sam wrinkled his nose. "*Now* he smells," he commented.

Anastasia picked the baby up.

"You have to be careful picking him up because he's so little," Anastasia explained. "See how I have to hold his back and head?"

Sam nodded. It *was* better than the dolls at nursery school. You didn't have to be careful with them. You could pick them up by one leg, or their hair, or even their clothes, if they were wearing clothes. You could drag them across the floor if you wanted. You could *throw* them if Mrs. Bennett wasn't looking.

He could tell that you wouldn't do that stuff with Alexander.

"Hand me one of those diapers," Anastasia said, gesturing toward the stack of diapers nearby. She laid Alexander on a padded table. Sam handed her a diaper and watched while she lifted the little nightgown and undid the diaper the baby was already wearing.

"YUCK!" Anastasia said loudly. Alexander stopped crying and looked at her.

Sam stood on tiptoe and peered at Alexander's bottom. He sniffed.

"Yuck," Sam said. "He pooped."

"I can't believe Mom loves the smell of babies," Anastasia commented as she cleaned Alexander carefully. She rubbed some lotion on his behind, attached a new diaper, and pulled his nightgown down.

"Did I wear a dress when I was little?" Sam asked suspiciously.

"Yeah, I think so. Sometimes, anyway."

"Gross," said Sam. "Did I poop in my diapers?"

"Yes."

"Gross," he said again.

Anastasia collected the warm bottle, settled herself in the rocking chair with Alexander, and fed him a little of the warm milk. He sucked for a moment, then spit the nipple out, burped loudly, spit up, and began to cry again.

"Did I —"

"Yes," Anastasia said.

"Gross," Sam muttered.

Anastasia propped Alexander against her shoulder and patted his back. He drooled on her sweater, grabbed her hair and tugged with one fist, and howled.

Anastasia rocked, patted, tried again to feed him some milk, and said a few baby-talk things, but Alexander paid no attention. He howled on. Sam watched. He listened. He sniffed now and then.

Finally Anastasia stood up. "Okay," she said. "Time for the Never-Fail Baby-Soothing procedure."

Sam followed her, noticing with surprise that she was going to the kitchen with Alexander in her arms. *Through* the kitchen. Into the laundry room.

Sam watched as his sister turned the dial on the dryer. He was very, very nervous. Sam had heard a terrible story once about someone whose *cat* got into the dryer.

"Anastasia," Sam asked loudly, "you're not going to *dry* him, are you?"

Anastasia chuckled. "Nope," she said. "Watch. Mrs. Parish taught me this." She turned the dryer on. Then she folded a baby blanket and laid it on top of the dryer. Finally she removed the howling Alexander from her shoulder and placed him, tummy down, on the blanket. He began to vibrate a little.

Within seconds his mouth closed. He put his bobbing head down. His eyes closed. His fists relaxed. The dryer hummed.

Alexander slept.

While Anastasia sat on a kitchen step-stool beside the dryer, watching Alexander vibrate and sleep, Sam trotted around the house collecting smells. He took a scrunched-up poop-smelling tissue from the wastebasket by the changing table in the baby's room. He picked up a scrunched-up spitup-smelling tissue from the floor beside the rocking chair.

He put both tissues into his Ziploc bag and closed it tightly.

When he got back home, he opened the Lab and looked the other way while he deposited the two tissues into the grape juice bottle.

"Gross," he murmured to himself, shaking his head. But it wasn't for him to decide, he knew. The gift was for his mother. And now he had two of her very favorite smells.

He was already wondering what the third should be.

4

"Sam," Anastasia said to her brother on Monday morning before she left for school, "listen to this. I changed the first part a little. And I added another line. Tell me what you think."

She had stopped by his bedroom on her way downstairs for breakfast. Sam was sitting on the floor beside his bed, trying to decide if his sneakers were on the correct feet before he Velcroed them closed.

He glanced quickly toward the Lab when his sister entered the room. The Lab was secret. He didn't want Anastasia — or anyone else — to know about it.

But Anastasia didn't even look at the Lab. If she

had, it would have seemed just like Sam's old toy-box to her. He had even sat some stuffed animals on its lid so that no one would suspect that secret stuff was taking place inside.

Anastasia was interested only in the paper that she had unfolded. She read aloud to Sam:

I'm glad that you are 38
I'm glad you're Katherine, not just Kate.
I'm glad our father is your mate.
I'm glad you have good body weight.

Sam gave his sister a perplexed, quizzical look.

She made a face. "It's not any good, is it? That last line, I mean."

Privately, Sam agreed with her. He thought the last line was terrible. But he didn't want to hurt Anastasia's feelings. He tried to tell her the truth in a kind way. "I don't exactly understand what it means," he said.

"Well, it means that Mom is a good size. Not too big, not too small."

"Why don't you say that, then?"

Anastasia frowned. "Because I want it to rhyme."

Sam examined his feet, decided that the sneakers were correct, and closed the Velcro fasteners. He stood up. "Why don't you just say that her size is really great? *That* would rhyme," he suggested.

Anastasia stared at him. She said the new rhyme under her breath, testing it out. Then she grinned.

"Attaboy, Sam!" she said, "you're a creative genius."

"I know," Sam said happily.

"But your shoes are on backward," she pointed out as she left the bedroom.

Anastasia had left for school, clattering down the back steps in her hiking boots and calling to her friend Meredith out on the sidewalk.

Sam's dad had left for work — he was a professor at Harvard University — muttering angrily at the car as he backed it out of the garage. Mr. Krupnik hated cars. He especially hated *their* car, which sometimes wouldn't start on cold mornings and which backfired noisily when it did.

Sometimes, when his dad was muttering about the car, Sam suggested that the Krupniks should buy a *new* car. All the guys at nursery school talked about Lamborghinis, and when they played cars they played Lamborghinis, saying "Rrrrrrrrr" loudly in their throats as they crawled across the floor.

Sam did not know exactly what a Lamborghini was, but he knew it was a good thing to have, so he had told his dad that a Lamborghini was what they should buy. His dad did not think that was a good idea.

Now that Anastasia and Mr. Krupnik were both gone, the kitchen was quiet. Sam's mom was busy at the sink, wiping the counter with a sponge. Sam, finishing a piece of toast and jam, peered through the window for his Monday carpool driver, his friend Leo Lizotta's mom. All the kids called her Mrs. Lasagna. She didn't mind.

"Would you like it if your name was Mrs. Lasagna?" Sam asked his mother.

She laughed. "No," she said, "because then I would be married to Mr. Lasagna. And I'd rather be married to your daddy."

"But if you had to have a *food* name, what food would you choose? I'd be Sam Egg, I think."

His mother squeezed the sponge, set it in the sink, and thought for a minute. "Let me see," she said. "I guess I'd be Mrs. Soup. Katherine Soup. Katherine *Chicken* Soup."

"Why?"

"Because I love the smell of chicken soup. It makes my mouth water to think about it. Maybe, if I have time, I'll make some chicken soup this afternoon."

Then she frowned. "Speaking of food, I'd better

37

get back to work on those cabbage drawings. I'm so sick of cabbages. And I *hate* the smell of cabbage soup."

"Here comes Mrs. Lasagna," Sam announced. He ran to the door. His mom leaned down to give him a kiss and ran her fingers through his hair. "Mmmmm," she said. "That new shampoo is nice. Your hair smells like —"

"Chicken soup?" Sam asked.

Mrs. Krupnik laughed. "No. Like newly mown hay in a sunny field. And maybe a wildflower or two. Plus the smell of little children's clean hair, of course. It's a wonderful combination."

Sam checked his pockets. He had a Ziploc bag folded in each one. These days, with such a complicated project, he needed a serious supply of Ziploc bags.

Trotting to Mrs. Lasagna's car, he tried to remember the smells his mother had mentioned. Chicken soup. That would be pretty easy — He'd just snitch some from the pot when she was making it.

Newly mown hay? Sunshine? Wildflowers? Where on earth would he get those things?

But then he remembered. His mom had said that clean *hair* smelled of those things. And hair was just about the easiest thing in the world to collect. Heck, all you needed was scissors.

Sam climbed into the back seat of Mrs. Lasagna's station wagon. He punched Leo hello, stuck his tongue out briefly at Jessica, and ignored Rosemary, who was in the front seat pretending to read a book about lions, even though everybody knew that she couldn't read at all yet; she still got her starting sounds all mixed up.

Sam buckled his seat belt, and Mrs. Lasagna headed to the nursery school.

Two hours later Sam found himself sitting in the big green time-out chair. He dangled his feet, swinging them back and forth, and sighed.

His dad had explained to him once that even grownups needed time-outs sometimes. In hockey games — grownup hockey games, with the Boston Bruins — the guys who behaved badly had to go sit in a special place. Sam had seen them on TV. The hockey players in the special place (they called it the penalty box) sat there looking mad, and they watched the clock to see when they could come out and play again.

It was the same at nursery school. Sam sat and sighed and looked mad and waited for the time to pass. He pretended that he was a Boston Bruin who had hit some other guy with his hockey stick and maybe knocked out his teeth.

"Okay, Sam," Mrs. Bennett said cheerfully after about a million minutes.

Sam climbed out of the green chair and pretended that he was skating into the game again, wearing his helmet and big gloves.

He skated carefully over to the art corner and sat back down at the table. He picked up the colored papers and crayons he'd been working with before he got into trouble and had to have time-out.

He noticed that Mrs. Bennett was watching him very carefully.

Nonchalantly, Sam began drawing balloons on his paper. He drew a red balloon and a green balloon and a pink balloon with a brown happy face in it.

Mrs. Bennett began helping another child work with clay.

Sam picked up the plastic scissors and began to cut out his balloons. Mrs. Bennett glanced over and smiled at him.

He smiled back. He was being good. He was only cutting out his balloons.

When no one was watching, he touched his own head behind his right ear, just to check it out. It didn't feel too bad. There wasn't a bald spot or anything. It wasn't like the time when he was younger (and therefore dumber, and therefore naughtier) and had cut *all* his hair, all over his head, and ended up looking like a porcupine.

This was just a small clump of hair, and Mrs. Bennett had gotten entirely the wrong idea because dumb Jessica had yelled and said that Sam was chopping everybody's hair off with the scissors, which was not true at all. It was only his own hair, and it was for a perfectly good reason, even though it was so secret that he had not been willing to explain it to Mrs. Bennett.

Somehow, with no one looking while he sat in the time-out chair, he had managed to get the little handful of hair into his Ziploc bag and safely into his pocket.

Sam sure hoped his mom would appreciate all the trouble he was going to for this birthday gift.

The soup was easy, just as Sam had imagined. It was simmering on the stove when he got home. And it *did* smell delicious. Sam, to be perfectly honest, had not agreed with his mother at all about the smell of babies. And he really wasn't much interested in the smell of shampooed hair. But the chicken soup aroma in the kitchen *was* wonderful.

His mother was in her studio. Sam climbed onto the kitchen step-stool very carefully, spooned some soup into his plastic clown cup, and then carried it

secretly to his room. He couldn't resist taking a little sip when it cooled, but he didn't eat it all.

With the door to his bedroom closed, Sam knelt beside his Lab. He took the bag of hair from his pocket, dropped the curls into the cup of soup, swirled the mixture around a little, and then added it — he didn't spill a drop, or a hair — to the large perfume bottle. He replaced the cap, tightening it carefully, and shook the bottle. The pipe made a clunking sound. The tissues that had contained the baby smells were now a dark purple mass on the bottom of the bottle. The hairs floated a bit, and he could see, holding the bottle up to the window, that he had captured two noodles from the chicken soup as well.

It was making a rather thick, and interesting, and *unusual* perfume, Sam decided.

It also didn't seem to smell very nice yet.

5

Tuesdays were boring. Sam didn't go to nursery school on Tuesdays. Some children did. Some children went every day. But Sam was a three-day-a-week person. So he went to nursery school only on Monday, Wednesday, and Friday mornings.

But Tuesdays were sort of boring.

"Can I — I mean, *may* I — go outside?" he asked his mother.

She looked up from the washing machine, which she was loading with blue jeans, and glanced out the window to see what the weather was like. "I suppose so," she said, "if you wear a jacket. And stay in the yard."

She helped Sam into his blue corduroy jacket

and opened the back door for him. "Do I have to stay in *my* yard?" he asked. "Or can, I mean may, I go into Gertrustein's yard?"

Gertrustein was their next-door neighbor. Her real name was Gertrude Stein, but Sam had always called her Gertrustein. She was one of his best friends, and often when he went to visit, she had just baked cookies to share with him. Sometimes she told him stories about when she was a little girl seventy-five years earlier, which she said was *almost* the same time as dinosaurs, although she had never seen any.

"Well," Mrs. Krupnik told him, "let me give her a call and see if she'd mind your dropping by."

Sam waited in his yard, fooling around with his tricycle. Anastasia had shown him how to attach a piece of cardboard to the wheel with a clothespin, so that it made a loud flippety noise when he rode fast. He rode up and down the driveway, pretending to be a race car driver in a Lamborghini.

"Okay, Sam!" his mother called from the kitchen door after a few minutes. "Mrs. Stein says she'd love to have your company!"

"Did she maybe just make cookies?" Sam asked.

"As a matter of fact, she told me that she just made *bread*!"

Sam made a face. "Not cookies?" he asked sadly. "Bread is boring."

His mother smiled. "Not homemade bread. There's nothing better than homemade bread. The smell of homemade bread is the most fantastic smell in the world!"

Sam climbed off his tricycle. He felt his pocket, just to be certain that he had one of his Ziploc bags. In the old days, before he had started work on his mom's birthday present, his pockets used to be full of interesting stuff: stones and marbles and paper clips and Matchbox cars and He-man models and broken crayons. Once, for a long time, he had carried around a piece of a jigsaw puzzle. At nursery school, the children were all working on a big, hundred-piece puzzle of a zoo scene. Sam wanted to be the person to put in the last piece, so he had — well, he hadn't really *stolen* a piece; he had *hidden* a piece — so that it would be the last one. He could tell, just by looking, that it was a part of the zebra.

But the puzzle had never been finished. There were about ten pieces missing at the end. Mrs. Bennett thought it was very mysterious, because it was a brand-new puzzle, and she said that maybe she would have to return it to the store and complain. She took it apart and put the pieces back into the box.

When he thought no one was looking, Sam returned his little piece of zebra to the box.

Later he saw Leo return a piece, too. And Adam. And Skipper. And Nicholas.

Sam sighed, thinking about his pockets and that they weren't very interesting anymore. He found the opening in the hedge that led to Gertrustein's yard and pushed his way through.

Then he remembered something. On the *other* side of Gertrustein's yard was the Sheehans' driveway, which contained the box of kittens.

Sam had told his mother that he would only go to Gertrustein's house and no farther. But if he stood with his feet in Gertrustein's yard, he could lean his head over to the Sheehans' driveway and just *look* at the kittens.

He decided to do that.

FREE, the sign still said. So they hadn't changed their minds. They were still giving those kittens away absolutely free.

From where he stood, Sam could see the big box and the sign, and he could hear the kittens. He could hear little mewing sounds. But he couldn't quite see them.

Guiltily, he edged his feet into the Sheehans' driveway just far enough so that he could peek into the box. Just for one *second* he would peek.

There were only three kittens left. One, the little

47

gray one, was curled up sound asleep. The two yellow ones were playing, wrestling with each other and jumping around.

Sam inched his feet a little closer. He reached down into the box with one hand and touched the sleeping gray kitten with a finger. Its fur was very soft. Its little head came up, the neck stretched, and the kitten yawned. It began to purr loudly as Sam's finger rubbed its head.

"Hi, Sam!" The voice startled Sam, and he looked up. Mrs. Sheehan was on her porch, holding her baby. The baby wasn't as small as Alexander. It was one of those babies that wears shoes and can walk already but isn't smart yet. One of those that you have to watch every minute or it would walk into the street and stuff. Its name was Kelly. Sam didn't know if it was a boy or a girl baby. There wasn't any way to tell, yet.

"Hi," Sam replied. He scurried back to the edge of Gertrustein's yard.

Mrs. Sheehan smiled. "A family came last night and took both the gray and white ones!" she said. "They had two little girls, and each one will have a kitten. They're going to name them Fluffy and Scruffy!"

"Oh," Sam said. He wondered who they were. He wondered who was so lucky that they could have two kittens of their own.

"That little gray one would be a great pet for you, Sam," Mrs. Sheehan said. "It's as friendly as can be."

"I know," Sam said. Under his breath, so Mrs. Sheehan wouldn't hear, he whispered sadly, "My daddy is 'lergic."

"Well, you think about it, okay? And don't forget — a free bag of cat food goes with each kitten!" She jiggled Kelly on her hip and turned to go back into the house.

Sam pecked into the box one more time and saw that the gray kitten had gone to sleep again. He scampered back across the yard and up the porch steps to ring Gertrustein's doorbell. As soon as the door opened, he knew that his mom had been correct about the smell of fresh bread. It was better than cookies.

"Butter? Or jam? Or honey?" Gertrustein asked. She was holding a piece of warm bread in one hand and a kitchen knife in the other.

Sam nodded with his mouth full. "Awvit," he said.

"*Awvit?*" Gertrustein looked at him, puzzled.

Sam swallowed hastily. "All of it," he said. "Butter. And jam. And honey.

"Please," he added politely.

49

Gertrustein nodded and began heaping butter, jam, and honey onto the bread.

One of the things that Sam liked best about his elderly friend was that nothing surprised her. She had explained to him that after a person is seventy years old, nothing surprising is left.

Sam was looking forward to that himself, although he had a few years to go, still.

"My mom said that homemade bread is the best smell in the world," Sam said.

Gertrustein thought that over carefully. "I think she may be right," she said finally. "But I have to admit that I love the smell of newly washed sheets that have hung on a clothesline on a very sunny, windy day in a yard where rosebushes are blooming."

"I never smelled that," Sam said.

"Well, I haven't either for a long time. My arthritis is so bad that I can't hang things outside, so I just put them in the dryer."

"So does my mom, and she doesn't even *have* arthritis."

"She's a busy lady, that's why. She has two children and a career. I'm going to send you home with a loaf of bread for her, Sam. Think she'll like that? I know she doesn't have time to bake."

Sam nodded. He licked the edge of his bread, where the honey was dripping.

"Here, let me show you something." Gertrustein got up from her chair. Slowly (her legs didn't work very fast because of her arthritis), she walked to the kitchen counter. She picked up a large blue bowl that was covered by a yellow dishtowel. She set it on the table in front of Sam.

"Are your hands clean?" she asked.

Sam looked at his hands. He tried to remember what they had touched lately. Tricycle. Doorbell. Kitten.

"Yes," he told her.

Gertrustein lifted the towel, and Sam looked at the pale mass of dough in the bowl. "That's bread dough," she explained. "It's rising, and I have to punch it down. Want to help?"

Sam nodded eagerly. If there was ever any kind of punching to be done, Sam wanted to be the one to do it. Punching bags? Pow! Pillows? Sometimes his mom wanted the pillows on the living room couch punched into shape. Pow!

Now bread. Sam was ready. He made his hand into a fist and went *pow* a few times in the air, practicing.

Gertrustein upended the bowl, and the dough fell onto the wooden table in a wonderful, soft

mound. She showed Sam how to punch it and watched while he used both fists enthusiastically. Then she loaded it back into the bowl and set it to rise again.

"It's the yeast that makes it rise," she explained to Sam. "It's really the yeast that makes it smell so good, too."

"What's yeast?" Sam asked, and Gertrustein showed him. It didn't look like anything much: just grayish-brown powder. But Gertrustein had said that the yeast made the bread smell good, so he knew it must be true. She sprinkled some into his hand and he sniffed it curiously.

He knew instantly that he needed yeast for his mom's perfume.

"Can, I mean may, I please keep it?" Sam asked shyly. He knew he couldn't just *take* it when she wasn't looking. Not from his good friend.

"Certainly," Gertrustein said matter-of-factly. So Sam took his Ziploc bag out of his pocket and shook the yeast from his hand into the bag. Gertrustein didn't even ask why.

Anastasia went to Sam's room that night to read him his story. His sister, mother, and father took turns putting him to bed. Sam liked that because they were so different.

His dad liked to read to him about scientific stuff: volcanoes, and dinosaurs, and racing cars and snakes. And his dad was especially good at reading poetry.

His mom absolutely refused to read anything that had snakes in it. But she liked happy stories about families and animals. Sometimes she read him books that had her name on the cover because she had done the pictures, and she sometimes pointed out things she wished she had done better. There was one very funny book about some children playing dress-up, and Sam's mom always frowned when she read it to him.

"See that, Sam?" she asked, frowning. "See how I have the little boy trying on the football helmet and the little girl pulling on the pantyhose? Why didn't I do it the other way, with the *girl* wearing the football helmet? Wouldn't it have been better if — "

Sam always turned the page impatiently so that she would go on with the story.

Anastasia was very good at reading scary stories. She could make her voice all spooky when she read, and sometimes Sam even had to pull the covers over his head just to hide, although he never wanted her to stop. Sam loved being scared.

Tonight she closed the door to his room when she went in and sat on the edge of his bed. "I want to consult with you again about this poem, Sam," she said.

Then she looked around and sniffed. "Something smells weird in here," she commented. "Do you smell it?"

Sam shook his head. He *did* smell it, but he didn't want to talk about it. The Lab was a secret. The perfume was a secret.

Gertrustein had told him that yeast makes the good smell happen. He had added his yeast that afternoon. He hoped the good smell would happen quickly.

"Read me the poem," he told Anastasia, just to change the subject.

She unfolded the paper, which was beginning to be covered with crossed-out lines. She noticed Sam looking at it and explained. "When it's finished, I'm going to copy it over on good paper, maybe in calligraphy, for Mom's birthday.

"Now. Listen and tell me what you think."

She read aloud:

I'm glad that you are 38.
I'm glad you're Katherine, not just Kate.
I'm glad our father is your mate.
Your size and shape are really great.

Although you don't earn a lot of money,
Your husband likes to call you Honey.
You have a daughter and a sonny
Who think your jokes are usually funny.

Anastasia looked at Sam. He looked back at her.

"A sonny?" he asked after a moment's silence.

She shrugged. "It rhymed," she said. But she wouldn't look at him, exactly. Sam could tell that she was embarrassed.

"Daddy doesn't call Mom Honey," Sam pointed out. "He calls her Katherine."

"Well, that rhymed, too," Anastasia said miserably.

Sam thought for a minute. He didn't want to hurt his sister's feelings. "You could say that she has a daughter and a son," he said, "and they think she's lots of fun. That would rhyme. And it would be *true*, too," he added.

"But what about the other two lines? I need two more lines in this verse. And they'd have to rhyme with *son* and *fun*."

Sam thought. He was getting sleepy. And his room did smell weird.

"I guess I could say I'm glad she's not a nun," Anastasia suggested.

"What's a nun?" Sam asked.

"No, wait! I've got it! I could say she's second to none!"

"Yeah, that'd be good," Sam agreed. "And then say she's the very best one. *One* would rhyme."

Anastasia stood up. "Thanks, Sam," she said. "I'll go write this down right away, before I forget. We only have a few days left. How's *your* present coming?"

Sam sniffed. "Okay, I guess," he told his sister. But he wasn't at all certain.

6

Sam dressed very quickly for nursery school on Wednesday morning. He woke up, took his pajamas off, dropped them on the floor, and jumped into his clean underwear, jeans, sweatshirt, and socks faster than he ever had before. He grabbed his sneakers and took them down to the kitchen, where his mom was fixing breakfast.

"My goodness, Sam," his mother said when he appeared. "I didn't even know you were up. Most mornings I have to shake you awake and then nag you and nag you to get dressed."

Sam climbed onto a kitchen chair and shook some Rice Krispies into a bowl. "Well," he explained, "today I was Mr. Speedo."

He didn't want to tell his mother the real reason that he had dressed so quickly.

Anastasia was gathering her books. "I'll be home late this afternoon, Mom," she said. "I have to stay after school to work on the newspaper.

"And Sam," she added, "it was really helpful, your suggestions last night. I worked on that project some more and it's coming along much better, thanks to you."

"What project's that?" Mrs. Krupnik asked. She went over to the table with her cup of coffee and sat down. She sliced a banana over Sam's Rice Krispies and poured some milk into his bowl.

"Secret," Anastasia told her.

"*Secret?*" Mrs. Krupnik said, looking puzzled. "I'm not sure I like that, Anastasia. Having secrets from your own mother."

Anastasia grinned. "Well, how about if it's a secret for a big event coming up this Friday evening?"

"Friday evening?" Mrs. Krupnik asked. Then she smiled. "Oh, I see. My birthday. I almost forgot. Well, okay, then. Birthday secrets are allowed."

Anastasia left for school, and Sam spooned up the rest of his cereal and bananas.

"I have a secret, too," he told his mother. "A

birthday secret. And so I don't want you to go into my room. Nobody can go into my room but me."

"But, Sam, what about your bedtime story?"

Sam thought. He didn't want to give up the nightly story. "We can read it downstairs, okay?" he suggested. "We can cuddle up on the couch in the study."

"Well, all right, I guess that would work," his mom agreed. "But, Sam, what about the laundry? I have to go into your room to collect your dirty clothes."

"I'll bring my dirty clothes down to the washing machine," Sam said. "But you mustn't go in my room. Promise?"

His mother chuckled. "Okay, I promise. But you have to promise to bring all the dirty clothes down. And you'll have to take the clean ones back up, too. Otherwise you won't have clean socks or undies."

Sam didn't actually care that much about clean socks or undies. He would have been happy to wear dirty ones every single day. But it was important to his mother.

And it was important to *him* that she not go into his room. It was the real reason that he had dressed so quickly this morning.

His room smelled *terrible*.

*

"Don't take your jackets off, children," Mrs. Bennett said. "Remember that today is a field trip? Who can guess where we're going today?"

"Circus!"

"Zoo!"

"Airport!"

"Disneyland!"

All of the children shouted their ideas. Sam listened eagerly. He liked every one of them. Sam loved field trips, although he had never quite figured out the name of them. When he was younger — when he had just begun to go to nursery school — he had thought that *field trip* meant that they would go to a field. He liked that idea just fine. He thought it would be fun to play in a field, run around a lot, maybe pick flowers, chase butterflies, and even see some cows and sheep up close.

But every time they had a field trip, Sam was surprised. They never went to a field at all — not even a baseball field.

Once they went to a bakery and watched guys in white suits make cupcakes.

Once they went to the Museum of Science and saw baby chickens coming out of eggs.

For a while he thought that maybe he had gotten the name wrong. Maybe it was actually *feel* trip that Mrs. Bennett was saying.

But no: they weren't allowed to feel the cupcakes. And they weren't allowed to feel the baby chickens.

So apparently it was just one more of those mysterious things that don't seem to make any sense. Sam had experienced a lot of those in his short life. It was like—he thought for a minute—well, like the word *litter*.

"Guess what! The Sheehans' cat had a new litter!" Anastasia had announced one evening a few weeks earlier.

But when Sam had gone with her the next day to see, he had expected the Sheehans' cat to be surrounded by crumpled paper and old Pepsi cans. He couldn't figure out why you would bother going to take a look at litter when you could see it anytime you wanted just by looking out the car window, especially in the corner of the park, where the wind blew things up against the fence.

But there was no litter around the Sheehans' cat at all. There were five kittens instead.

Thinking about that this morning made Sam feel a little sad. He was thinking of the gray kitten curled in a ball, sleeping, and the way it had purred when he stroked its head with his finger.

Dumbo. That's what he would name that kitten, Sam decided, because it was gray and had big ears. He would name it Dumbo for sure.

If it belonged to him.

*

Today's field trip was to the Boston Aquarium. Several mothers were coming along as helpers and drivers. Sam watched carefully while Leah's mom folded up Leah's wheelchair and loaded it into her station wagon. Just a couple of days before Sam had shown Leah how to clothespin a flippety-flippety piece of cardboard onto one of her wheels so that she could be a Lamborghini. He watched to be certain that the cardboard didn't get knocked off.

Sam had been to the Aquarium before and had seen the dolphin show and the hammerhead shark. That was his favorite, the hammerhead shark, even though it was *very* scary to look at. It had mean eyes on each side of its big, square hammerhead.

And he loved the penguins, who looked like pudgy, serious, little men waddling around in black and white suits. One of Sam's very favorite books was called *Mr. Popper's Penguins*. Sam felt as if he wouldn't mind being a penguin himself, because they seemed to have fun all the time. They could swim with their hands at their sides so that they looked like torpedoes. Then they got out of the water and stood around looking at each other between swims.

So he was very glad to be going to the Aquarium again to see all of his favorite things and to have his hand stamped by the man at the front door. It made you feel very important to have your hand stamped.

But he was a little concerned about something. He knew that the Aquarium was an important part of his special perfume, because his mom had said many times that the smell of the sea was one of the absolutely best smells in the world.

The Boston Aquarium definitely smelled of the sea. And Sam had one of his Ziploc bags folded, as always, in his pocket.

But he couldn't figure out how to collect a bit of the sea.

The Aquarium was very large, and today it was crowded with children. There were groups from schools, like Sam's, with teachers and mothers telling the children again and again to stay together and hold hands. There were parents pushing strollers and pointing out fish and sharks and turtles to babies who were sucking pacifiers and looking sleepy. There were teenagers wearing Walkman radios and dancing a little bit to music that no one else could hear.

In the center of the Aquarium was the enormous glass tank that stood as high as a tall building. The people walked around it on the slanted walkway, going up and up, higher and higher, and looking through the glass as they went. That's where you could see the hammerhead sharks, and the giant turtles, and a billion other fish that would swim right up close to the glass so that you could see every bit of them: their eyes and flippers and fins and teeth and —

"Look," Sam said to Mrs. Bennett, pointing. "That fish has whiskers!"

"My goodness," Mrs. Bennett said. "Maybe it's a catfish!"

Sam thought it was really weird that some fish had whiskers. It made him think of kittens, and then that made him think of the little gray kitten, and he decided that he would not name it Dumbo at all; he would name it Whiskers.

If it belonged to him.

Sam's pal Adam poked him and pointed up toward the top of the tank. "Scubaman!" Adam said. "I'm gonna be that when I grow up!"

Sam looked up through the green water and saw a diver, with his helmet, tank, and lines, swimming down through the fish and sharks with a pail of food.

"Me too," Sam said to Adam. "I'm gonna be that, too." But it was a scary thought, being a diver who went into the tank where hammerhead sharks lived.

His class continued walking up on the circular walkway. Sam patted his pocket and his Ziploc bag. He knew that when they reached the top of the huge tank, they would be able to look down into it. Maybe then he could carefully, while no one noticed, dip his bag into the tank to collect some sea.

But the thought made Sam very nervous. He would be reaching into the place where hammerhead sharks lived. They would be able to see his hand with their mean, glittery eyes.

He wished that he had a metal diving helmet for his hand.

"Okay, guys," Mrs. Bennett announced. "Let's detour over here instead of going all the way to the top."

"Over where?" Sam asked.

"To the tidepool area," Mrs. Bennett explained, leading the way. "Because here you can actually touch things if you're very careful. And the Aquarium lady will tell you all about the little creatures that live in tidepools, like starfish."

The children followed Mrs. Bennett, who was pushing Leah's Lamborghini wheelchair, and gathered around the little tidepool where a woman was talking about starfish and anemones.

They could put their hands right in, and there was not a single hammerhead shark.

"Don't mash it!" Leo scolded Rosemary, who was

holding something wet and glistening. "Mrs. Bennett, she's mashing it!"

"Am not!" Rosemary said loudly, and put the glistening thing back.

Sam touched a starfish and a clam, and he thought maybe he touched an eel, but he wasn't certain, and it slithered away from him. The water was cool and the rocks were slippery; the entire tidepool smelled as much like the sea as the whole sea itself.

He looked around. The Aquarium lady was talking, and most of the children were paying attention to her. Mrs. Bennett was also listening to the Aquarium lady. Leo was examining the underside of a starfish, and Leah was making her fingers walk along the rim of the tidepool area. No one was looking at Sam.

Carefully he opened his Ziploc bag. Pretending that he was listening attentively to the Aquarium lady, he silently dipped the bag into the tidepool and brought it out. He had just enough water — and a couple of bits of seaweed captured by mistake.

He turned his back so that no one would see, sealed the bag, and stuffed it back into his pocket.

Much later, helping the kids into the van, Mrs. Bennett gave Sam a gentle shove on his behind.

"Oh dear, Sam," she said to him privately in a

quiet voice, "you're a little bit damp, I'm afraid."

It was true, although it was not what Mrs. Bennett thought.

"It's okay," Sam told her. "I don't mind."

At home that afternoon, he added sea to the perfume. He did it very quickly, with his face turned aside, because the smell was very strong now, and getting worse.

And he noticed that something else was happening to the perfume. It was making a noise. It was bubbling, each little bubble coming to the surface and popping in a tiny, explosive sound.

Quickly he replaced the cap on the bottle and put it back. He closed the top of the toybox and knelt beside it for a moment with his ear against the wooden side. He held his nose and listened.

Blup. Blup. Blup.

Sam left his bedroom nervously. He was beginning to be a little frightened of his perfume.

Later that afternoon, when his mom thought he was playing in his sandbox, Sam crept over to the Sheehans' driveway again, to peek at the kittens.

One more was gone, one of the yellow ones. Now there were only two kittens left: one yellow, one gray, both of them snoozing together in a corner of the box.

Mrs. Sheehan came down the driveway with Kelly in a stroller.

"Hi, Sam!" she said cheerfully. "Only two more to go!"

"Did somebody take the other yellow one?" Sam asked. "Some little kid who needed a pet?"

Mrs. Sheehan laughed. "Yes," she said, "only it wasn't a little kid. Do you know Mr. Leggett, who lives down the street in the brown house?"

Sam nodded. "The old man," he said.

"That's right. He lives all alone. When he was out for a walk the other day, he saw the kittens and decided that a kitten would be good company. He chose one of the yellow ones. He named it Blondie."

"That's a pretty good name," Sam said.

"They've all found good homes so far," Mrs. Sheehan said. "I suppose those last two will, also."

"I suppose so," Sam said sadly.

"Of course, that little gray one would just *love* to be yours, Sam."

"I know it would," Sam whispered.

He waved good-bye to Mrs. Sheehan as she headed off toward the grocery store. Then he trudged back to his own yard, thinking of the kitten. He would name it Sleepyhead, he decided.

If it belonged to him.

7

When Sam set out across his yard on Thursday morning, he realized that he was going to do a very naughty thing. But it was his mother's fault, he explained to himself.

I shouldn't be doing this, he thought as he passed his sandbox and his tricycle. His walking slowed a little.

But just last night at dinner, Mom —

Sam remembered what his mom had said at dinner, and he continued on through the yard.

Here is what his mom had said: "Sometimes, if you're feeling depressed, you have to do something really crazy to cheer yourself up."

*

Mrs. Krupnik had been explaining at dinner why she had gone to the beauty parlor that afternoon and gotten her hair cut very, very short.

Sam liked his mom's new haircut.

But Anastasia, when she came home from school, had shrieked, "MOM! What have you *done* to yourself? You look like Arnold Schwarzenegger!"

Sam didn't know what she meant. "Who's Arnold Schwarze ——" But he couldn't pronounce it.

"You know, Sam," Anastasia said. "The guy who was the Terminator."

Sam didn't know. But he liked the sound of that guy. And he liked his mom's haircut.

Sam's dad, when he came home from work, had dropped his briefcase on the kitchen floor in surprise. "Katherine!" he had said in a very shocked voice. "Where's your hair?"

"Mom turned into Arnold Terminegger," Sam had explained. "I mean Schwarzinator."

Mr. Krupnik wasn't listening to Sam. He was simply staring at Katherine Krupnik's head.

That's why Mrs. Krupnik had explained and explained, all through dinner. "I'm about to be thirty-eight years old," she said, "and that's depressing, because it seems *ancient* to me."

72

"It isn't ancient," everyone reassured her, but you could tell that she didn't believe them.

"And the publisher called and said that they want those snail drawings completely redone," Mrs. Krupnik said with a sigh, "because the author decided to change the main character to a *slug,* which is not at all the same as a snail —"

"Slugs are gross," Anastasia commented. "They're slimy and repulsive."

"I know that," her mother said. "That's why I was depressed. I'm getting old, to start with, and on top of that, for the next two weeks I have to replace all those cute little snails with fat, glistening, repulsive slugs. I sat there this morning trying to draw slugs, feeling sorry for myself, and finally I decided I needed to do something completely crazy just to cheer myself up. So I called Verna at the beauty parlor, and she had a little time available after lunch, and —"

"And you had yourself turned into the Terminator," Anastasia said in an amazed voice.

Mrs. Krupnik ran her hand over her cropped head and grinned. "Right," she said. "And it did cheer me up. Don't worry, guys, you'll get used to it. And it'll grow back in no time.

"I *thought* about having it all shaved off," she added cheerfully.

Sam gulped. He wondered what it would feel

like to have a bald mom. He already had a bald dad.

Now, the following morning, Sam remembered what his mom had said: that sometimes you need to do something crazy if you're feeling depressed. That sounded completely true to Sam.

And Sam was certainly a little depressed. The smell in his room was stronger than any smell that he had ever experienced. And the noise from his Lab was louder; it bubbled and spurted constantly. Once, visiting the Museum of Science with his family, Sam had seen a movie about volcanoes that had scared him so much that he had slept in his parents' bedroom that night. His mom and dad had assured him that there were no volcanoes in Massachusetts.

But now he had created something that *sounded* like a volcano, at least, even if it wasn't one. And not only was it in Massachusetts — it was right in his own town, in his own room, in his own toybox. And no one knew about it but Sam.

He didn't know what to do, so he had done nothing. He simply hoped that it was all a normal part of perfume-making, and that by Friday evening, in time for his mom's birthday party, the noise would have subsided, the smell would have changed, and the perfume would be ready.

But in the meantime he thought about his mom's advice for people who were feeling depressed.

Do something a little crazy, she had said.

So Sam continued walking across the yard.

"Good morning, Mrs. Sheehan. I came for the little gray kitten, and don't forget you said I could have cat food, too," Sam said loudly and very rapidly when Mrs. Sheehan answered his knock on her kitchen door.

"Hi, Kelly," he added, when he noticed the baby clinging to Mrs. Sheehan's leg. Kelly grinned and drooled.

Mrs. Sheehan smiled at Sam. "Well, I'm just delighted that you and your family decided on that, Sam," she told him. "I know that little gray one will be a wonderful pet for you. Are you sure you don't want his brother, too?"

Sam shook his head. "No," he whispered. "I can only have one."

"Well, I'll get him for you. They're in the dining room. I brought their box in for the night, and I haven't put them out yet this morning. I hope I haven't missed any customers!" Mrs. Sheehan, with Kelly toddling behind her, disappeared into the dining room while Sam waited in the doorway. She was back in a moment with the gray kitten; she placed it carefully in Sam's arms.

Sam looked down happily. It was the first time he'd actually held the kitten. But it was just the way he thought it would be: soft and warm and sleepy. The kitten wiggled a little in his arms, re-arranging itself, and began to purr.

"Do you think you can carry the food, too, Sam? Or should I come with you and deliver the food to your mother? I could leave Kelly in the playpen for a couple of minutes."

"I can carry it," Sam said hastily. Mrs. Sheehan tucked the bag of cat food under his left arm and watched while Sam, holding the kitten and the food carefully, made his way back down the steps.

Very quietly he walked back across his own yard and up his own porch steps. Very quietly he crept into the hall and sneaked up the back stairs. Very quietly he opened the door to his room.

"Sam? Are you in your room?" his mother's voice called.

"Yes," he called back. "But don't come in!"

"I won't. I promised you I wouldn't. Bring your dirty clothes down to the kitchen when you can, though!"

"Okay," Sam agreed. He laid the kitten gently on his unmade bed. Still half asleep, it wriggled until it found a comfortable spot against his pillow.

Sam sat on the edge of the bed and watched his new pet sleep. Its tiny whiskers moved faintly as it breathed.

His mom was right. It *did* cheer you up to do something crazy, Sam decided.

Very quietly he gathered up his discarded pajamas and yesterday's underwear from where they lay in a wrinkled heap on the floor.

Then he headed downstairs to help his mom do the laundry. Now and then, secretly, to himself, Sam smiled.

From time to time during the day, Sam crept into his room to check on things. The kitten seemed happy. It didn't seem to mind the smell in the room.

He made a bed for the kitten in a corner of the room, on a soft pink towel that he borrowed from the linen closet. He poured some cat food into a small bowl and some water into another. The kitten had nibbled a bit and lapped a bit and slept a bit.

He gave the kitten some toys: a tennis ball borrowed from his father's gym bag and a small ball of blue yarn borrowed from his mother's knitting.

He filled the empty shoebox from Anastasia's closet with sand from his sandbox and set it on the floor. To his surprise, the kitten seemed to know exactly what it was for.

Sam thought it was quite interesting that the kitten was exactly the same age as the baby, Alexander, but it seemed a whole lot smarter.

He checked on the perfume, too. But nothing seemed to have changed. Apprehensively, Sam picked up the bottle and held it toward the window so that light shone through. He could see all sorts of things floating in the murky purple liquid: Kleenex shreds, tobacco flecks, seaweed, strands of hair, noodles, and the outline of his father's pipe at the bottom.

The bottle felt warm, which surprised him.

And it continued to fizz and bubble.

That evening after supper, Sam helped his sister bake a birthday cake for their mother. Anastasia measured the ingredients into the large mixing bowl, and Sam stirred carefully. Now and then he licked a little from the spoon.

"Cooking's neat," Anastasia commented. "It's almost like magic."

"What do you mean?" Sam asked. He watched some melted chocolate blend into the yellow mixture of flour, sugar, and eggs as his spoon went around and around in the bowl.

"Well," his sister explained, "each of those things by itself is nothing. Flour, for instance: boring. Sugar: boring. Butter —"

"Boring," Sam said.

"Right. And eggs, and baking powder. All of them boring. But then you put them together — and presto!"

Sam giggled. "You get *cake!*"

"Well, of course you have to bake it," Anastasia said. "I shouldn't have left that part out. But the point is: if you know the right stuff to put together, you can make something wonderful out of a whole lot of nothing stuff!"

"Just like perfume," Sam said.

"Here, let me stir for a minute. It really needs to be beaten pretty hard." Anastasia took the bowl and spoon from Sam and began to beat the cake batter. "What do you mean, like perfume?"

Sam bit his lip. He sort of wanted to tell his sister about what he was doing up in his room, and about the strange smell and the noise from the container. But he wasn't certain that he should.

"Well, I mean that you take a whole lot of nothing stuff, like Kleenex and noodles and tobacco,

79

and if you put it together just right, you can get wonderful perfume!" Sam reached over and smeared his finger in a puddle of thick batter that had dropped on the table. He licked his finger.

Anastasia set the bowl down and tapped the spoon handle on its rim, to drop the batter from the spoon into the bowl. "I can't remember if I added the vanilla," she said, frowning.

Sam shrugged. He couldn't remember, either.

Anastasia uncapped the little brown bottle. "Well," she said, "I'll add some. If I already put it in, then the cake will have a little extra vanilla. It won't matter. Vanilla's one of the best flavors in the whole world. Here: smell." She held the tiny bottle under Sam's nose. He sniffed and grinned. His sister was right. That was just about the best smell *ever*.

Anastasia tilted the bowl and began to pour the batter into the cake pans that she had greased and floured. "What were you saying about noodles and tobacco?" she asked.

Sam watched her as she used a rubber spatula to scrape the last of the batter from the bowl into the baking pans. When he was certain that she wasn't paying any attention to him, he put the little bottle of vanilla into his pocket.

"Nothing," he said. Suddenly Sam was feeling better about his perfume. It needed vanilla, he decided. Once he got the vanilla into it, it would be okay.

"Open the oven door for me." Anastasia picked up the two pans filled with batter and waited while Sam, wearing a potholder mitten, pulled the oven door open.

"There," Anastasia said as she set the oven timer. "You just wait, Sam. In about half an hour this kitchen is going to smell *fabulous!*"

"You just wait, kitten," Sam said later. Holding his breath so that he wouldn't have to inhale the hideous smell, he opened his perfume bottle and poured in all the remaining vanilla. "In about half an hour this room is going to smell *fabulous!*"

The kitten, who had no name yet, wiped its face with one paw, tilted its head, and watched. Its small pink nose twitched.

8

Early in the morning, Sam crept out of his bedroom in his pajamas and closed the door quietly
behind him. It was barely light. No one else was
awake yet. The kitten was sound asleep on its towel
bed in the corner of Sam's room.

But Sam had had a bad night. He had had bad
dreams. Usually, if he had a bad dream, he could
call out, even in the middle of the night, and his
mom or dad would come. If his dream was about
monsters, they would turn on the lights and show
Sam that there was nothing scary in the closet or
under the bed. Sometimes they would sing a funny
song with him, about monsters, and then he could
go back to sleep.

But last night Sam had had bad dreams, and he couldn't call for anybody because he didn't want anybody to come to his room when it was so full of secrets.

So he woke in the night and lay there in the dark, smelling the hideous smell and listening to the horrible bubbling, popping noise from his toybox.

Sam felt very, very sorry for himself. He had done something crazy, and it hadn't helped, not really.

Finally, when it was beginning to be light, he tiptoed down the hall in his bare feet. He went into his parents' bedroom and stood there silently by their bed, watching them sleep.

His dad slept on his back with his mouth open and snored a little. His dad was bald on top, but he had shaggy, curly hair around the back and sides of his head which turned into a beard in front. Sam reached up and stroked his dad's soft, shaggy hair gently. But his dad didn't wake up.

Sam crept around to the other side of the big bed, where his mom slept on her side with her mouth closed in a little smile. She snored just a teeny bit, too. Sam reached up and stroked his mom's new Terminegger haircut; it felt like touching a hairbrush. Katherine Krupnik didn't wake up.

Finally Sam went to the foot of the bed and climbed up over the patchwork quilt that was folded there. He burrowed up the middle of the bed, between the mounds of his parents' bodies, until he found a snuggly spot, just big enough, there in the middle. He curled up into a ball.

"Hi, Sam," said his dad's sleepy voice. "Don't freeze. Get under the covers."

So Sam climbed in under the covers to exactly the place he wanted to be. He curled up into a ball again.

"Attaboy, Sam," said his mom's groggy voice.

This room smelled wonderful. It smelled of Mom and Dad, and clean sheets and old quilt, and sneakers on the floor and briefcase on the chair; it smelled of clock-radio and books and lamp and curtains, and of a painting of trees that hung on the wall between the windows.

Now Sam was able to sleep without dreams.

When the alarm buzzed, all three of them woke up and yawned. One giant yawn from Myron Krupnik, one medium-size yawn from Katherine Krupnik, and one small yawn from Sam Krupnik.

"Just like the Three Bears, right, Sam?" his dad asked as he stretched.

Sam giggled. He liked the idea of being Baby Bear.

"What day is today?" asked Sam's mom sleepily. She sat up.

"Friday," Sam's dad said. "I have to teach a Shakespeare class at ten o'clock." He sat up, too, and yawned again.

Sam, still lying in the center of the bed, raised one arm high and moved it rapidly in the air. He made a rattling noise with his mouth. His parents both stared at him.

"I'm Shakespeare," he explained. "I'm shaking a spear. An imaginary one."

"Oh," said his mom.

"Oh," said his dad.

They could hear Anastasia coming down the stairs from her third-floor bedroom. In a moment she appeared in the doorway, still wearing the giant T-shirt that she wore to bed instead of a nightgown. Anastasia had many different T-shirts with things written on them; some of them were ordinary things, like RED SOX. But this one was not ordinary, and it was one of Sam's favorites, because all the words were easy ones, and Sam could read it by himself. This T-shirt said: ARE WE HAVING FUN YET?

Sam always answered that question when he saw that T-shirt.

"Yes," Sam said in a loud voice and kicked off the covers, "we *are* having fun!"

"What are *you* doing in here?" Anastasia asked. She squinted at him. She hadn't put her glasses on yet.

"He's just visiting," Mrs. Krupnik explained. "I guess he got lonely in the night."

Anastasia yawned. "Well," she said, "happy birthday, Mom."

Sam, who had forgotten the importance of the day, repeated, "Happy birthday, Mom!"

Myron Krupnik, who had also forgotten, said, "Happy birthday, Katherine!"

And Katherine Krupnik, who had forgotten as well, flung herself back on the bed with a stricken look. "Thirty-eight," she moaned. "Pull down the shades so that no one will see my aged face and body. Call the drugstore, Myron, and see if they can supply a walker. Or a *cane*, at least.

"Throw away those sneakers on the floor over there," she added. "The ones I wore yesterday? And have the shoestore send over a pair of lace-up old-lady shoes with arch supports!

"And what else?" she went on in a mournful voice. "A dress. Yes. I need a flowered silk dress. I can never wear my jeans again, now that I'm old. Get me a crocheted shawl, too."

Sam laughed, even though he didn't have the

slightest idea what arch supports were. He could picture the lace-up shoes and the flowered dress and shawl and cane.

"Mom," he reminded her in a loud voice, "you *can't* be old, because you got a Terminegger haircut!"

Katherine Krupnik reached up and felt her head. She brightened. Finally she smiled and sat up again. "You're right, Sam," she said. "Thank you for reminding me."

Anastasia padded off to the bathroom to brush her teeth. Sam's dad went into the other bathroom and Sam could hear the shower start.

"Better start dressing, Sam," his mom told him. "It's a school day."

Sam sighed.

"Need some help?" she asked. "I'd be happy to go to your room with you and help you find your clean clothes."

Sam sat there on his parents' bed, his legs dangling off the edge. He thought about how nice it would be if his mom could come to his room. His room would be neat and clean; it would smell good, and his toybox would have nothing in it but toys. She would help him find some nice, clean, sweet-smelling socks, and maybe she would play trucks with him for a few minutes. They would crawl around the floor side by side, pushing their vehicles, and saying "Rrrrr" the way they did when they played trucks together. The only sound in Sam's room would be the "Rrrrr" of their two voices, and there would be no horrible, scary, bubbling sound, and —

"Sam?" his mom asked again. "Do you need some help getting dressed?"

Sam shook his head slowly. "No," he said gloomily, and slid down off the bed.

Are we having fun yet? he asked himself as he trudged down the hall to the closed door of his bedroom.

No, he answered himself silently. We sure *aren't*.

Anastasia took Sam aside privately before she left for school.

"The cake's all set," she told him. "It's on a high shelf in the pantry, and Mom swore a solemn oath she wouldn't look.

"And Dad'll be home early — he promised — and he's bringing flowers. And scrod, too. He's picking up fresh scrod at the fish market because it's Mom's favorite dinner."

"Did Daddy make Mom a present?" Sam asked.

Anastasia shrugged. "He told me he did, but he sounded kind of embarrassed about it. I think maybe it didn't turn out real good."

Sam was silent. He knew exactly how his dad felt. It was a feeling much, much worse than embarrassed.

"I know how he feels," Anastasia said, almost as if she had read Sam's mind, "because my poem is really not turning out too great. Do you mind helping me some more with it?"

"Nope," Sam said. It felt good to be able to help someone. "Read it to me."

Anastasia took the paper from her bookbag, unfolded it, and cleared her throat. "I'll read the whole thing, okay? Even though you've already heard the first part?"

"Okay," Sam said.

Anastasia read aloud:

I'm glad that you are 38.
I'm glad you're Katherine, not just Kate.
I'm glad our father is your mate.
Your size and shape are really great.

You have a daughter and a son
Who think you are a lot of fun.
As mothers go you're second to none
In fact you are a perfect one.

Sam grinned. He liked Anastasia's poem now. In the beginning he had thought it was sort of stupid, but she seemed to have gotten the hang of it.

90

"It's good," he told his sister.

"Wait," she said. "It's the next verse I'm having trouble with. I wrote this last night. Listen." She began to read on:

Your favorite food is broiled scrod.
You never ever are a clod.
Your haircut is a little odd.
It doesn't seem to match your bod.

Sam cringed.

"It's awful, isn't it?" Anastasia wailed. "I *knew* it was awful!"

"We can fix it," Sam told her. "It just needs a little fixing."

"Sam!" Mrs. Krupnik's voice called from the kitchen. "Hurry up, sweetie! Your carpool's here!"

Anastasia looked at her watch. "I gotta go, too," she said. "I'm going to be late for school. I don't know when I'll have time to fix it, Sam," she added in a dejected voice. "The birthday party's *tonight!*"

"SAM!" his mother called again.

"Coming," Sam called back. He trotted off down the hall to get his jacket and say good-bye to his mom.

Anastasia was right. Time had pretty much run out.

9

Sam helped his mom that afternoon as she cleaned up the first floor of the house and set the table in the dining room for dinner.

"You shouldn't have to clean up for your own birthday party," Sam told her. "You should make us do it."

But Mrs. Krupnik laughed and said she didn't mind. "Anyway," she pointed out, "Anastasia isn't home from school yet, and neither is your dad." She looked at her watch. "They should both be here pretty soon, though. How are we doing with the table? About finished?"

Sam looked at the dining room table. Usually the

family ate in the kitchen, but this was, of course, a special occasion.

They had set five places because Gertrustein was coming for dinner. It had only taken a few minutes to arrange the placemats — Sam had chosen his favorites, the yellow ones with blue flowers — and the silverware and plates.

But then Sam and his mom had spent at least an hour figuring out how to fold the yellow napkins so that they looked like swans. Mrs. Krupnik had a magazine article with instructions. But it was hard.

"I could make them into hats," Sam muttered as he tried for the millionth time to make a swan.

"I think I could make them into snails or slugs," his mother said. "Shall we give up?"

"Let's try one more time," Sam said. So Mrs. Krupnik read the instructions one more time, very slowly, folding as she did. Sam folded his at the same time. "Corner B halfway in so that it is perpendicular to side two —"

Finally they each had a swan — a little wrinkly, a little misshapen, but a swan nevertheless.

Carefully they made three more before they forgot how. They set a yellow swan on top of each dinner plate. Mrs. Krupnik said that that was how they did it in fancy restaurants.

Sam had never been to a fancy restaurant. His

favorite restaurant was Chuck E. Cheese, and he also liked the Ground Round okay. But neither of those places had napkins folded into swans.

"I think it's all ready," Sam said, looking at the table. "We have to leave the middle empty because Dad's bringing flowers."

"And fish," his mother said. "Gosh, I hope he doesn't forget the scrod. Everything else is ready: salad and potatoes and veggies. Mrs. Stein said she'd walk over around six o'clock. She's bringing some nice fresh rolls."

"I hear the car," Sam announced. "Dad's home."

The car clattered into the driveway, its engine sputtering, and they could hear it backfire after it entered the garage. In a moment they heard Myron Krupnik slam the garage door.

Sam's mom giggled. "That's the only time your dad ever gets mad," she said. "He really hates that car."

"I saw him kick it once," Sam told her, "but he hurt his toe when he did. Then he said the S word."

"Well," Katherine Krupnik said, "if I ever get rich, I'll buy him a new car for his birthday."

"A Lamborghini," Sam suggested.

"Anybody home?" Anastasia's voice came from the kitchen. "Me and Dad just got here at the same time!"

"Dad and I," Mrs. Krupnik called back, correcting her. "We're in the dining room. Come see how the table looks, all set for the party!"

Anastasia, her arms full of books, came to the door of the dining room. She looked at the table. "Neat," she said. "And Dad has flowers for a centerpiece.

"But what did you do to the napkins?" she asked, puzzled.

"Guess," Sam said.

"Can't you tell what they are?" Mrs. Krupnik asked.

Anastasia walked around the table slowly, examining the napkin swans. Finally she shook her head.

"Sailboats?" she guessed uncertainly.

"*Rats,*" Mrs. Krupnik said. "After all that work."

"They're supposed to be rats?" Anastasia asked. "Why on earth would you want rats at your birthday dinner?"

"No, no," said her mother. "I didn't mean that they were supposed to be rats; I meant —"

"Hi, guys," Myron Krupnik said, appearing at the dining room door. He held a bouquet of flowers wrapped in twisted green tissue paper. "Hey, great — I got just the right color. Yellow chrysanthemums — they'll go with the napkins. What did you do to the napkins?" He peered at the table.

"Oh," he said politely, "that's really clever, folding them into the shape of mushrooms."

Mrs. Krupnik and Sam looked at each other and sighed. Silently they collected the napkins and began to fold them into boring rectangles.

"I want to talk to you guys before dinner," Mr. Krupnik said in a serious voice to Anastasia and Sam. "Can we meet privately in my study?"

"About what?" Anastasia asked. "Are we in some kind of trouble?"

"No," her father reassured her. "But we need to talk about the birthday gifts."

For a moment Sam, in the fascination of folding napkins and the anticipation of a party dinner, had forgotten about the *gifts* part. Now his heart sank. There really was no time left. If his perfume hadn't turned to perfume by now — or didn't turn to perfume in the next hour — he was in serious trouble.

"I need to check on something," Sam said. "I'll be back in a minute for the meeting."

He scooted up the stairs to his room. But he knew it was no use. He knew it before he opened the door, and he *certainly* knew it after he opened the door, because the smell almost knocked him down. The kitten, hearing him, looked up with its head turned sideways as Sam entered the room. It came to him and rubbed itself against his leg.

"Poor kitten," Sam murmured. "Do you feel okay? It really smells yucky in here."

The kitten seemed all right, but Sam was worried. He remembered that once, a while ago, he had felt just fine one day, but the next day he itched all over and his head was hot, and he had chicken pox. Things like that could take a person by surprise.

So Sam decided to move the kitten to a new location, one with fresh air, before it was too late. Stealthily he crept down the hall to the guest room, making several trips, with the kitten, its towel bed, its food, bowl, sandbox, and toys.

He patted its head, apologized to it for the move, and went back downstairs.

While Katherine Krupnik busied herself in the kitchen, Sam and his sister and father met privately in the study.

Myron Krupnik, sitting at his desk, spoke in a very solemn voice. "I have to tell you kids," he announced, "that I really tried very hard to follow your mother's wishes, which were, as you know, to have homemade birthday gifts."

"Me too," Anastasia said gloomily.

"Me too," Sam said nervously.

"But," their father went on, "I am, frankly, not

97

very good at arts and crafts. And so, while you kids were working hard and turning out nifty gifts for your mother —"

"*Hah,*" Anastasia whispered.

"*Hah,*" Sam said under his breath.

Their father didn't hear them. "I was *trying* just as hard as you did, I think. But — well, this is hard to admit — I made a real botch of it."

He reached over and picked up a large wrapped package that was leaning against the bookcase. He looked at Anastasia and Sam. "I am very, very embarrassed about this," he said. "It's *horrible.*

"I'm going to unwrap it and let you see it, and I'll understand when you laugh, but I want you to promise that you'll continue to love me even when you see what a mess I made of your mom's birthday gift." Looking absolutely miserable, Mr. Krupnik began to untie the knot in the string.

"Wait, Dad!" Anastasia said.

Her father looked up.

"Before you unwrap it, Dad," Anastasia said, "I want to tell you that you're not the only one. I'm not much good at that stuff, either, and I tried, but I really made a mess of my present, too. And I'm just as embarrassed as you are. Sam's the only one who succeeded in making Mom a great gift. Mine's in my bookbag. Wait, everybody, and I'll get it and bring it in here and show it to you, so you don't have to feel bad. And Dad, I'll understand when you laugh, but you have to promise that you'll still love me, even when you see what a mess *I* made."

Anastasia started toward the door.

"Wait!" Sam said in a loud voice.

His father and sister stared at him, and he scrambled down from the couch. "You get yours, Anastasia," Sam said. "And Dad, you bring yours. And both of you come to my room so I can show you mine."

"You mean we finally get to see the big secret you've been working on in your room?" Anastasia asked.

"Yes," Sam told them. "And I'll understand when you laugh, but you have to promise that —"

"We'll love you anyway," his father said, smiling.

"Okay," Sam said. "You'll get to see it. And hear it. And *smell* it."

10

"We'll be down in a few minutes, Katherine!" Mr. Krupnik called. "We have some last-minute birthday things to attend to!"

"We won't be long, Mom!" Anastasia called. They were standing in the upstairs hall, outside Sam's room. Mr. Krupnik held his large package under one arm, and Anastasia had her green notebook in her hand.

They could hear Mrs. Krupnik down in the kitchen, where she was arranging the yellow flowers in a vase. "Okay!" she called back cheerfully. "Don't be long, though! Mrs. Stein will be here soon!"

Carefully, as if the door might be holding back

a ferocious monster, Sam turned the knob. Then he pushed the door open very slowly and stood aside so that his father and sister could enter his room.

His father coughed.

Anastasia made a gagging sound.

Both of them blinked in confusion.

Sam, by this time, was so accustomed to the condition of his room that it no longer surprised him. But he tried to imagine how it might seem to people entering for the first time.

The smell was overwhelming. It smelled like —

Well, Sam couldn't even describe *what* it smelled like.

"What do you think it smells like?" he asked his father and sister nervously. Somewhere, way back in his imagination, a tiny bit of hope still lingered. He hoped that just maybe his father and sister would say, "It smells like the finest, most unusual perfume in the whole world. The finest perfume ever invented."

Myron Krupnik sat down on Sam's bed with his package on his lap. He considered Sam's question carefully, sniffing occasionally to test the scent again as he thought. Now and then he coughed.

Finally, he said, "Once, in 1981, I attended a conference in New York during a week when the New York garbage collectors had been on strike

101

for seventeen days. So garbage was piled up in the streets. It was August — very hot.

"Just outside my hotel, in front of a Thai restaurant, was a particularly awful pile of green plastic garbage bags. They had split open, and the stuff had oozed onto the sidewalk, and flies had laid eggs on it, and the eggs had hatched, and — are you sure you want to hear this?"

Sam shook his head. "I don't think so," he said.

Sam's dad reached over and took Sam's hand, to show that they were still pals. "Anyway," he said. "This smells like that."

Sam, holding his dad's hand, looked at Anastasia. "What do *you* think it smells like?" he asked miserably.

She had been thinking. "Well," she said finally, "once, at school, an eighth-grade girl named Martha Holmes was coming down with the flu. And after lunch she felt really crummy, like she was going to throw up. And she was standing in the hall, in front of her locker, with the locker open, and she felt embarrassed because everyone was walking past—even *boys* — and so she stuck her head inside her locker and barfed egg salad sandwich and tomato soup and chocolate pudding on top of her gym suit and a math book. Then she closed her locker and locked it and went right home and didn't come back to school for five days.

102

But on the fourth day, when she wasn't back yet, the principal told the janitor to open up the locker because everybody was noticing that *something* was wrong, and —

"Are you sure you want to hear the rest of this?"

"No," said Myron Krupnik firmly.

"No," said Sam in a small voice.

Anastasia reached over and took his other hand, to show that they were still pals.

"Anyway," she said, "this smells like that."

The three of them sat silently for a moment. They breathed little choking breaths. No one even said anything about the sound — a sound like bubbling lava — that was coming from the toybox.

"Sam," his dad asked at last in a sympathetic voice, "what is it?"

Sam tried to speak very matter-of-factly. Though it wasn't easy, he tried to use a brave and self-confident voice.

"It's perfume," he told them, "Homemade."

"I see," Mr. Krupnik said after a long silence. "Well, I can't sit in here very long because it's tough to breathe. But I promised I would show you mine."

He untied the string around his package.

"Let me explain it before I show you," he said.

"First of all, I used my favorite photograph of your mom — a black-and-white one where she was wearing a sweater, and her hair, back when she had long hair, was blowing in the wind. Remember that picture? I had it framed, and it was on the desk in my office?"

Anastasia and Sam nodded. They had both visited their dad's office at Harvard, so they knew the picture he was talking about.

"Well, I had that photograph enlarged until it was enormous. Poster size. Then I glued it to a piece of plywood so that it was nice and sturdy. Then I borrowed some paints from my friend Morris Castillo, who teaches in the Art Department. And in the hours when I wasn't busy teaching or grading papers, I worked on *painting* that photograph.

"I was going to make it into a gorgeous portrait," he said unhappily. "I wanted to show her beautiful blue eyes, and how the sunshine made golden streaks on her hair, and —"

He sighed and looked miserably at the package still on his lap.

"Show us, Dad," Anastasia said sympathetically.

"Yeah, show us," Sam urged.

Mr. Krupnik slid the picture out of its paper wrapping and stood it against the side of the toybox where they could see it.

Sam gulped. It was terrible. *Scary.* It looked like a Wild Thing from one of his favorite books. It was almost as terrifying as a hammerhead shark.

If it were hanging on your bedroom wall, Sam thought, you would never *ever* be able to close your eyes and go to sleep.

He glanced at his sister. Her mouth was open in astonishment as she stared at the hideous painting.

"What does it look like to you guys?" Mr. Krupnik asked. And Sam knew — because Sam had experienced it — that deep down in his dad's imagination was one teeny-weeny bit of hope that maybe the painting was okay after all.

They didn't answer for a moment.

Finally Anastasia said, "Dad? You know what it looks like? Once this eighth-grade girl at school, Martha Holmes, barfed egg salad sandwich and tomato soup on top of a green gym suit —"

Sam began to giggle. He didn't want to hurt his dad's feelings, but he couldn't stop giggling.

He looked over and saw that Myron Krupnik's shoulders were shaking, and he realized that his dad was laughing, too.

Anastasia halted her description. She picked up her green notebook and opened it to a folded piece of paper. When she unfolded the paper, Sam could see that Anastasia had used her calligraphy pen and lettered her poem carefully onto the page.

"Here's mine," Anastasia announced. She began to read.

Sam had heard the poem before — all but the last part that Anastasia had added only that afternoon — so it didn't really surprise him anymore. He watched his father's face. His father was an expert on poetry. He taught poetry at Harvard. He *wrote* poetry that was published in books, and people — sometimes people who didn't even know his father — bought the books.

Anastasia read aloud:

I'm glad that you are 38.
I'm glad you're Katherine, not just Kate.
I'm glad our father is your mate.
Your size and shape are really great.

You have a daughter and a son
Who think you are a lot of fun,
As mothers go you're second to none.
In fact you are a perfect one.

Your favorite food is broiled scrod.
You never ever are a clod.
Your haircut is a little odd.
It doesn't seem to match your bod.

You don't like mice or rats or bugs
But for money you paint slugs.
I hope you like your birthday cake.
And that your stomach will not ache.

Anastasia looked up. Very slowly she folded the paper. But instead of returning it to her notebook, she leaned down and placed it in front of her father's painting, which was leaning on the toybox.

Then, in a very grown-up and dignified voice, Anastasia said, "I know it's not very good. But please feel free to tell me what you think."

Sam could tell, watching her, that Anastasia, like himself and his father, still had a teeny bit of hope about her poem. Sam didn't say anything but watched his father. His father had once won the National Book Award for a volume of poetry. Sam didn't know what the National Book Award was, but he knew that it was important, and that his father was important, at least in the world of poetry.

Mr. Krupnik cleared his throat. Then he said, very slowly, "Once, in 1981, I attended a conference in New York. It was a hot week in August and the New York garbage collectors had been on strike for seventeen days. And in front of a Thai restaurant, near my hotel —"

Anastasia started to giggle.

So did Sam.

Their father did, too.

The three of them — Myron Krupnik, Anastasia Krupnik, and Sam Krupnik — laughed and laughed. They sat side by side on Sam's bed in the most foul-smelling room in Massachusetts, looking at the worst painting in Massachusetts and the worst poem in Massachusetts, which were both resting against the only toybox in Massachusetts that made a rumbling, spurting sound that, as they laughed, grew louder and louder.

They were still laughing when the perfume exploded.

11

Myron Krupnik used the corner of Sam's sheet to wipe the thick purple liquid from his beard and mustache.

Anastasia used Sam's pajamas to clean her glasses, which were coated with purple and had flecks of tobacco stuck to the lenses.

Sam couldn't see at first. Then he realized that his eyelashes were coated with small soggy clumps of purple Kleenex. Bits of seaweed and noodles slid down his forehead and cheeks.

No one spoke for a moment. Then Mr. Krupnik said in a very serious voice, "It may be that what my painting needed was a little more purple."

Sam looked, after he got the last of the Kleenex

out of his eyelashes, at his father's painting. The thick perfume liquid slid slowly in purple streaks down his mother's face, across the bright blue eyes that his father had painted, and into smears on the red-painted sweater.

Anastasia leaned down and picked up what was left of her calligraphed poem. It was a limp, wet sheet of purple paper now, and the ink had run in black curlicues across the page.

"Greatly improved," she commented cheerfully, and wadded the paper into a ball.

It was amazing, Sam thought, how much better he felt. All week, when his perfume had been brewing, he had felt more and more scared and uncomfortable.

But now, when his room was ruined, when his wallpaper was splotched with purple and his hair was dripping with noodles and he had baby-poop in his eyelashes, and his dad's painting had turned into a giant smear, and his sister's poem was gone entirely, reduced to a little wet spitball, *now* he felt wonderful.

Sam grinned, looking at his wrecked perfume.

He noticed that his father, looking at his ruined painting, had a cheerful smile.

And Anastasia, too, holding her destroyed poem in her wet, purple hand, was absolutely beaming.

The three of them sat happily and silently for a minute.

Suddenly, they heard Katherine Krupnik's voice coming up the stairs and through the door.

"Are you guys about ready?" she called. "Mrs. Stein's here! Myron, you promised you'd grill the scrod! What's holding everything up?"

Their grins disappeared.

"We just need a few more minutes!" Mr. Krupnik called down to his wife. But he looked panic-stricken. There were still purple streaks dripping in his beard and huge splotches on his shirt.

"Bathroom!" Anastasia ordered. "All of us. *Quick.* Soap and water! Clean shirts!"

They scurried around, gathering shirts, running water in the bathroom, scrubbing the purple from their faces and hands. They moved in fast-motion like an old Three Stooges movie, when Larry and Curly and Moe would go in and out of doorways, bumping into each other with little yelping sounds.

"Now," Anastasia said when they all had clean faces and clean shirts and freshly combed hair, "what on earth are we going to do about a present?"

Her father shook his head in despair. "We blew it," he muttered.

"I know," Sam said suddenly. The idea had

come to him exactly the way ideas come in comics, when a light bulb appears over someone's head.

They looked at him suspiciously. "No arts and crafts," his dad said. "Please. We don't have the time."

"And let's face it," Anastasia added, "we don't have the talent."

"Nope," Sam promised, shaking his head. *"Listen."* He whispered his idea to them.

They listened, at first with surprise, then with interest. They asked a few questions, made a few suggestions, and agreed that it was not only a good idea, it was a great idea, and they had just enough time if they hurried.

"Attaboy, Sam!" said his sister and father together.

"That was a wonderful meal, Katherine," Mrs. Stein said, wiping her mouth with her napkin. "Or perhaps it's you I should say that to, Myron, since it was you who broiled the fish."

"And it was Anastasia who baked that delicious cake," Mrs. Krupnik pointed out.

"Sam helped," Anastasia said.

"And you made the rolls, Gertrustein," Sam pointed out. "With *yeast,*" he added.

Katherine Krupnik smiled. She looked at the birthday cards, including the one that Sam had made at nursery school, which were propped up in a circle around the flowers in the center of the table. "I have such a wonderful family," she said. "That includes you, of course, Gertrude," she added fondly, patting Mrs. Stein's hand. "We think of you as one of the family.

"I don't even mind being thirty-eight anymore," she went on. "Now that I've been thirty-eight for a whole day, I'm getting used to it. It feels okay."

"Your haircut helps, of course," Anastasia pointed out.

"It certainly does, Katherine," Mrs. Stein agreed. "I'm thinking of getting one just like it myself."

"Thank you," Mrs. Krupnik said, and ran her hand over her bristly hair.

Mr. Krupnik rose from his chair at the end of the table and tapped on his coffee cup with a fork.

"Speech, speech!" said Anastasia.

Sam wiggled in his chair with excitement. He knew that they were going to give the present now.

His father beckoned for Sam and Anastasia to come and stand with him, one on either side.

Sam felt very proud to be part of such an important ceremony. He practiced his part in his head and hoped that he would remember to say it correctly. They had had only a very few minutes to memorize their parts.

And Sam knew that his was the most important part.

Mrs. Krupnik and Mrs. Stein were both watching with interest, smiling and waiting to see what would happen.

"Ready?" Mr. Krupnik whispered to his children. They nodded. "Okay, go ahead." He nodded at Anastasia, who was standing on his right.

Anastasia cleared her throat, straightened her shoulders, and spoke her lines in a clear voice.

Because we could see that you needed a lift,
We looked all around for a lovable gift —

She looked at her dad and nudged him a little with her elbow to remind him that the next lines were his. He cleared his throat and straightened his shoulders.

It comes with free food and it doesn't have fleas,
And though I'm allergic I'll try not to sneeze —

Myron Krupnik looked at Sam, who was already standing very tall and straight, waiting for his turn, the most important part.

Sam leaned down, reached under the table, and lifted the box that was waiting there. He handed it to his mother, who lifted the lid and then gave a startled chuckle as the kitten popped its gray head up and looked around.

Finally Sam said his lines:

It was all my idea, so I'll take the blame.
And if you just ask me, I'll tell you his name.

His mom was smiling and stroking the kitten's head with her finger. She looked over at Sam quizzically.

"Tell me, Sam," she said.

Sam beamed. "Purrfume," he announced proudly.

Read more about
the hilarious adventures of
Anastasia
and her adorable brother, Sam!

Now on sale from Yearling Books
wherever paperbacks are sold.

Anastasia krupnik

LOIS LOWRY

ISBN: 0-440-40852-0

Anastasia Krupnik

To Anastasia Krupnik, being ten is very confusing. For one thing, she has this awful teacher who can't understand why Anastasia doesn't use capital letters or punctuation in her poems. Then there's Washburn Cummings, a very interesting sixth-grade boy who doesn't even know Anastasia's alive. Even her parents have become difficult. They insist she visit her ninety-two-year-old grandmother, who can never remember Anastasia's name. On top of all that, they're going to have a baby—at their age! It's enough to make a kid want to do something terrible. If she didn't have her secret green notebook to write in, Anastasia might never make it to her eleventh birthday.

ISBN: 0-440-40100-3

Anastasia's Chosen Career

Anastasia Krupnik has exactly one week to work on her school assignment called "My Chosen Career." Determined to be a bookstore owner, she must first develop poise and self-confidence. So Anastasia takes the plunge and spends her life savings on a modeling course at Studio Charmante.

She has one week to interview a bookstore owner, write a report, and complete her modeling course. Luckily, her new friend Henry is with her most of the way. Is Anastasia destined to be a successful bookstore owner or a glamorous model? Only Anastasia has the answers!

ISBN: 0-440-40291-3

Anastasia on Her Own

Help! Anastasia Krupnik's mother must organize her chaotic life. So Anastasia, who is a very organized person, and her father invent the solution to Mrs. Krupnik's problem: the Krupnik Nonsexist Housekeeping Schedule.

But when Mrs. Krupnik goes to California on a ten-day business trip, Anastasia finds that the problem isn't solved at all. It's hard to stick to a schedule that doesn't leave room for her little brother, Sam, who's come down with the chicken pox, and her father's former girlfriend, who's invited herself to dinner. How is Anastasia supposed to cope with these interruptions when she's planning her first dream-date dinner for Steve Harvey?

It's a cinch. As long as she sticks to the Krupnik Romantic Dinner Week Schedule, what could possibly go wrong?

ISBN: 0-440-40087-2

Anastasia Has the Answers

Humiliated. That's how Anastasia feels whenever she tries to climb the ropes in gym class. How come everyone else can climb those hateful ropes?

Since Anastasia has decided to become a journalist, it should be easy for her to answer most questions. Then why can't she understand about Daphne Bellingham's parents' divorce? And why can't she please Ms. Willoughby in gym class?

Finally Anastasia thinks she has the answers! When a team of foreign educators visits her school, she plans a big surprise that will amaze her classmates, Ms. Willoughby, and the visitors.

all about Sam

LOIS LOWRY

ISBN: 0-440-40221-2

All About Sam

Everyone knows Sam Krupnik. He's Anastasia's pesky but lovable younger brother.

This is Sam's big chance to tell things exactly the way he sees them. He has his own ideas about haircuts, nursery school, getting shots, and not eating broccoli. Sam thinks a lot about being bigger and stronger, about secret codes and show-and-tell.

Make way for your little brother, Anastasia. Here for the first time is Sam Krupnik's story. What a life!

attaboy, Sam!

LOIS LOWRY

ISBN: 0-440-40816-4

Attaboy, Sam!

Sam Krupnik is at it again. This time he wants to make a special surprise perfume for his mother's birthday. First he has to collect his mother's favorite smells in Ziploc bags. He uses an old grape juice bottle to hold everything from chicken soup to his father's pipe to a poop-smelling tissue from a baby's room.

Sam stashes all the smells in his toybox and won't let his mother into his room. It's really starting to stink in there. Still, Sam can't wait for his mother to see and smell her birthday surprise. But Mrs. Krupnik isn't the only one who's in for a surprise.